I0581706

HEARTS & STONES

M M WONDERLAND

KNIGHT KING PRESS

Text copyright © 2025 by M. M. Wonderland. All rights reserved.

Cover art copyright © 2025 by M. M. Wonderland. All rights reserved.

No part of this book may be reproduced in any form or by any electronic or mechanical means, including information storage and retrieval systems, without written permission from the author, except for the use of brief quotations in a book review.

No part of this work contains text or images generated by AI or large language models.

Knight King Press & M. M. Wonderland forbid the use of their copyrighted images, text, and material of any and all kinds to train and/or influence AI, LLMs, or future technology.

Power to the artists.

To my Pa-pa & Ma-ma, for instilling in me a love of cards.
"Hearts made of stone. doodly-whop. doodly-whop."

To my sister, without whom this would never have been written.

Show me a hero and I'll write you a tragedy.

— F. SCOTT FITZGERALD

PART ONE
THE BATTLE

I have seen many types of hearts:
Gold, gem, fire, and ice.
But mine is lost to me
I wish I could cry for it, wish I could kiss his lips,
But I have lost that option and I died that day.
So remember, child, remember, dear person
who finds these words hidden in my notes:
Hearts & stones will hurt your soul,
but love will break your mind.
-The Queen of Wonderland

ONE

"Chess is such an odd game."

"You're only saying that because you're losing."

Lamprocapnos S. Heart sat up, shook out her ruby red curls, and glared at her adviser.

Mack Hatter XVII, son of Mack Hatter XVI—the current head advisor to the King of Hearts—barely even looked up. "Oh please, don't act like a child."

"She can't help that." Rudyard, the Prince of Hearts, sat primly in a rocking chair, reading a book of nursery rhymes that he could recount in his sleep.

Lam fell back onto her stomach across the chess board from her opponent. "I am a child."

"For all of two more years." Mack moved his rook and took her last bishop.

"Now, really—" Her curse was muffled in politeness and the click of her queen being moved.

"What did you say, dear Princess?" His lips twitched upwards as he took the queen that she had just moved. Mack was one of the smartest people in all the kingdoms and the third most mad, well...maybe fourth.

Lam picked up his king and turned it in her hands. "Chess is subpar. It doesn't make any sense. They're just stones."

A breeze blew in the open window, making Rudyard shiver. "Don't go saying that at the ball tonight."

Fingers tightening around the body of the white king, Lam sighed before setting it down and patting its head. She wanted to be civil, to respect the neighboring Kingdoms of Wonderland, to not redraw the line that was broken with the looking-glass wall. "But you can do so many things with just one deck of cards," Lam threw up her hands and her hope of being respectful, "so many games and arrangements. With chess, it's all the same over and over and over."

Lam sighed, ignoring Rudyard's glare and Mack's hum of thought. She hated war, but these annual games seemed worse—a temporary calm.

Oh, of course they weren't really at war, but the borders kept changing and patience wore thin. And then there were the games the nobles would play, often with the loss of life and limb. Her father, the King of Hearts, had lost his right leg and her mother, the Queen, had lost her right ring, middle, and pointer fingers. So far, Rudyard had no permanent injuries, but how long could that last? At seventeen, this was his second Games, and he only had one more before he would become a full jack.

Lam flopped onto her back, letting out a sigh. "I'm tired of games." She twisted to glare at the chessboard. "That means you, chess."

A soft knock came at the door, and Lam looked up to see her head maid. "My lady, it's time to get dressed."

"Is it time already?" Mack sat up, pulling from his left pocket a white gold watch. He frowned, turning it upside down and tapping it with his middle finger. Seeming unsatisfied, he pulled a second from his waistcoat's breast pocket, this one a plain gold. Again, he frowned and tapped the watch. He pulled a third from his orange braid. The final timepiece seemed the only one to tell the correct time. "It seems so." Mack stood and held out a hand. "Have fun, Rudyard, Lamprocapnos. And try not to insult the entire Board of Chess."

Taking his hand, Lam smiled. "I will try." Then she turned and followed the maid to her dressing room as Rudyard stretched and went back to his book.

THIS WAS HER FAVORITE PART—NOT just the gowns, but the idea that in the span of one day she could be a sword fighter, a student, and a princess.

But also the gowns.

That day, it was one of the Hatters' creations, specifically Mack Hatter XVI. Lam stood in the middle of the mirror-lined room as her maid layered her with short, black petticoats and chatted about all the things she hoped would be at the ball and how much she wished she could go. From behind one of the sliding mirrors, she pulled the over skirt: a brilliant red silk, beaded with black swords and bloody hearts. Both girls oohed and aahed and the maid insisted on Lam doing a spin.

"That's a right beauty, Miss." The maid's hands went to the back and smoothed down a section that had flipped. "Even if it is a little short."

It was true, the dress was one of the shortest Hatter had made for her, ending a little above the knees. Dress styles were still mostly long, but shorter and shorter dresses were getting more and more popular.

"Well, I like it." Lam grinned as she gave another spin.

After that, the maid produced a red bodice with cap sleeves that was structured by black boning. She laced it up, cinching in the princesses curves. Lam had a classical hourglass figure, built equally from muscle and natural form.

"Now," the maid took Lam's hand and helped her from the stool, "I'm sure Hatter wants to see how it turned out."

Skipping back to her room, Lam found Hatter holding a box under one arm and staring at the watch on his wrist.

"Hatter, I love it!"

"Of course you do. I made it." Hatter smiled at her, eyes twinkling. He was a tall, middle aged man with bright orange hair and slightly sunken cheeks. "But that's not even the best part."

From the box he pulled out his newest creation with his long, bandaged fingers. Lam couldn't help smiling, too. It was a crown made of gold cards in the shape of a top hat.

"Hatter!" she laughed, "You must be mad if you think I can wear that."

"I prefer the term *'dangerously creative,'* and you must wear it, because I told you so."

"But how?"

"Like this," he said, revealing a headband.

It was much lighter than she expected and the headband was almost unnoticeable in the waves of her playing-card-red hair. They had decided to leave it down and let it form its perfect, upside-down hearts.

Lam looked around. "Now all I need is—"

"A pair of shoes." Hatter finished, holding out a pair of black velvet shoes with a solid ruby heel and long red, lace-up ribbons that had also been in the box.

Lam smiled up at the man who had partially raised her. "How do I deserve you or your work?"

"You don't," he knelt down before her, "but I'm here to stay." He, in turn, smiled up at the girl whom he had partially raised. "Now give me your foot."

LAM'S HEELS clicked on the red marble stairs leading from the Castle of Hearts' twin stained glass doors. The glass depicted Hearts' entire history, from when the Storytellers of Adventure, Mystery, and Revenge first formed the Deck of Cards.

The night was frosty and she couldn't help shivering and pulling her fur stole tighter around her bare arms. It was still the early part of spring and winter clung to the nights. Her gaze rose from the steps to the large, ornate carriage that would take her and her family to the ball. It was gold and birch, its pumpkin shape modeled after the one that Queen Ella had taken to the King of Diamonds' party all those years ago, though this one was powered by modern engineering.

As her shoes sank into the plush carpet, Rudyard started to laugh. "You look madder than Hatter."

"Well at least I look like myself. You look like you're suffocating."

"And I am!" Rudyard said, tilting his head back and raising his eyebrows as his thin circlet, lined in ruby, slid to his nose. It was rare to see him in a full suit, much less one so lavish.

Hands shaking a bit, Lam sat down next to her father. She was thankful that not only were The Games held in Cards that year, they were held in their own Kingdom of Hearts as well. That only happened every eight years and Lam couldn't help feeling a little special.

"You both look lovely." Their Mother leaned over from where she sat next to Rudyard and patted Lam's cheek. "I'm so proud of you." Her dark red eyes stared into Lam's with a deep warmth that filled Lam like a fire. The Queen's mechanical fingers were gold today, as they were most of the time, but now they were complimented by the swirling filigree of her gold crown. The curling pattern was mimicked in the fabric that made up her bodice and cape sleeves. The skirt held the same movement, though it was from the thick layers that were now taking up a third of the carriage.

"Thank you, Mama!" Lam grinned, even as her mother frowned.

"I told you, you should call me Mother. It's more elegant." Not being royal by birth, the Queen was far more concerned with appearing so.

The King leaned over in his jeweled, red suit. "Oh, darling," he put one hand on her neck and pulled her cheek to his lips, "let her call you Mama." His eyes were the same bright red as Lam and Rudyard's, and now shining with joy. "I find it adorable."

Grinning wider, Lam stared out the fogging window. But still, as the carriage glided into place outside the ball, Lam felt like all of her organs were either on the ground or in her throat.

"Your Highnesses," the footman bowed, "we have arrived."

THE BALLROOM WAS STUNNING, made specifically for this event with velvety black curtains, red, black, and gold wallpaper, a red and black checkerboard floor, and enormous, graceful chandeliers hanging from the ceiling. It came as little surprise to Lam when she noted there was no white in the whole room. But there were people in white—the people from the

Kingdom of White Chess, shining in their dresses and finery. A slight cough from behind made her realize she wasn't moving. With a soft nudge on her arm from Rudyard, she began to walk down the stairs.

Ridiculously, she wished her skirt was longer and crown not so large. For just a strange moment she wished she wasn't so bold. But then, she thought of Hatter and held her head up high.

"Presenting the King and Queen of Hearts and their contestants: Rudyard M. Heart, and his sister, Lamprocapnos S. Heart."

Rudyard was confident as he walked down the stairs. "Just remember, you're not the only one who's new."

"I'm not scared!" Lam was annoyed at the tremor in her voice.

Rudyard raised one eyebrow slightly and looked at her out of the corner of his eye. "Tell that to the heart beating in your throat."

"It's not."

"Your face is red."

"No it's not!"

"Your legs feel like pudding."

"No they—!"

"Your hands are trembling."

"N—" She looked down, her hands were shaking so much that she couldn't hold her brother's arm.

Rudyard turned to her, stepping back. "All you have to do is socialize with people who may or may not kill you."

"And you're really helping." Lam puffed out her cheeks and glared.

He smiled and bowed. "Here to serve."

Then he melted into the crowd and Lam was alone among enemies. Lam felt surrounded, caged. She was not very tall, but everyone from Chess was. She tried to smile at some of her friends from the other Kingdoms of Cards, but she couldn't catch anyone's eye.

"Presenting the King, Queen, and Crown Prince of White Chess, and their contestant, Adelyn W. Queenside."

Lam's eyes were drawn up to the royal family. Their skin shone in the crystalized light from the chandeliers; their hair the closest to pure white she had ever seen. Some said they were descended from Blood Weavers, who were as white as snow from their tongues to their hearts. As she stared at the princess, she thought it could be true. Adelyn was the same age as Rudyard, though she had only made it past the first challenge last year. Her brother, on the other hand, was the only current prince to have graduated from The Games and become a full heir.

Lam was about to turn from them when the prince caught her eye. His hooded gaze pricked her skin and pulled a shiver up her spine. A smile twisted his lips the barest bit before he looked away and returned to his resting glare. A memory, as sharp as the shattered tea cup, was trying to burrow into her mind and bleed out all her waning confidence. Lam shivered at the look and the memory, turning from both to the rest of the crowd.

She decided that the food table was the safest place. As she approached, she saw three girls she would have preferred to avoid. The triplet sisters of Diamonds were not bad people, to the extent that anyone can be called not bad, but they were not fun to be around. Delicately nibbling on pastries and cookies, the sisters stood around in their overly bejeweled dresses, chatting about things of little importance.

One of them, Farren, caught sight of Lam through the crowd and called, "Oh, Lamprocapnos, come and chat with us!" She spoke with the cheerful tone of a child spotting their friend, but her eyes were as cold as ever.

Lam could not blame her for this; it was said that the girls were born with hearts as hard and unfeeling as the gems of their country, and Lam believed it. Her steps were smooth as her shaking subsided, once again just a princess at a ball.

"Farren, Faina, Fern, I hope I find you are well."

"Yes, indeed!" Fern tossed one of her long, blonde braids over her shoulder, letting her peppy tone fill in for the lack of feeling in her smile. "We have been talking of small things, but with you here, we can talk of grander things!"

Faina nodded emphatically, twisting her curls though her fingers, trying not to disturb the strings of jewels layered in her hair.

Lam let herself smile a little. "Well now, I do not know what you might mean."

"The Games!" the girls chorused.

Still one year too young, the Princesses of Diamonds were hungry for news. Before, Lam had been like them, theorizing on what the tasks would be and who would win. But now it felt strangely hollow, like guessing what will happen to the woman who broke a mirror, or the boy who walked past the black cat.

Lam hummed softly. "I'm afraid I know no more than you."

The girls sagged. Fern was the first to rally. "Well, if you have no news of the future, than perhaps you can tell us of the past!"

"Oh, yes!" Faina looked back to Lam. "I would love to know how Jewels Week went in Hearts."

Glad for a topic that she enjoyed, Lam relaxed. "It was lovely, as it is every year. Only this year, it was even more extravagant. And cold." She could still remember the snow decorating her cheeks as she paraded though the streets, tossing gems correlating to the day to the subjects by the road. "On the last day, the sun came as well, boding good things for this year."

Farren forced her face into a pout. "That's no fair, its our holiday and we didn't even see a ray of sunshine the entire time." She shook her head, looking down and seeming to notice Lam's dress for the fist time. "My," her eyes rose back to Lam's, driven wide in a mask of surprise, "you're brave to wear such a dress."

Lam felt a twist in her gut at the phrasing but only let a kind smile pull her lips. "Why, thank you. I do find it makes me feel more free."

Fern giggled, one of the few things the girls could do genuinely. "Yes, it is lovely, but I would have chosen a smaller crown."

"Ah, but it compliments the simplicity of her hair so well." Faina had no emotions in her eyes, but she let a smile play on her lips. "When you leave it down it looks so..."

"Carefree?" Farren offered.

Lam's smile became more strained. This was the main reason she didn't like talking to the triplets. When they were entertained, they were kind, as kind as sunshine, but if bored for even a moment, they could be as cruel as the salt mines in their homeland.

"Carefree! What a lovely word to describe her."

Lam was suddenly no longer part of the conversation, but just a talking piece, as the pastries had been till they were turned to crumbs.

"Lamprocapnos was a carefree girl," Faina broke into rhyme, smiling at Lam with emerald eyes, "She would move and dance with a twirl. Some called her lucky, some called her luck. But everyone knew she was quite stuck."

Fern took up the rhyme, making the next stanza, "Lamprocapnos was a wild thing. Crowned in cards and covered in rings. Some called her silly, some called her small. But no one could ever know her at all."

Farren laughed and wrote a final stanza with her brightly painted lips, "Lamprocapnos was kin to a Queen. Bright and shining, but rarely seen. Some called her quiet, some called her meek. But really she was just never allowed to speak."

The three girls burst into laughter and Lam flushed red. Making up rhymes had always been their main pastime, yet they had only become rude as they got older. Lam had been the victim of many of their poems, but they never ceased to annoy and amaze her every time.

Lam brought her hands together, smiling with the practiced grace of the kin of a queen. "Bravo!"

The triplets bowed, and laughed, and wandered off, still chatting over the lines.

"Why do you put up with it?"

Lam spun to see a boy standing next to her, only feet away, grabbing tarts by the handful.

It was rare to meet someone she'd never seen before. To be perfectly honest, she wasn't great with faces or names but she was sure she would have recognized him. He was not very tall, only a little taller than her, with bright cyan hair and a suit that, depending on the light, looked either black or cyan.

He certainly didn't fit the color scheme of the event. In truth, *nothing* about him fit anything in the Kingdoms of Wonderland.

"Well—" Lam tripped over her words, "They're princesses, I—"

The boy turned to face her, two tarts in his mouth and three more in his hand. Her eyes rose to his. They were the eyes of a cat and the color was... it wasn't changing, but it was like when you look at a kaleidoscope and you keep changing the way you see it. One moment it was green, then orange, then pink...

He seemed just as shocked at her staring at him as she was to see his eyes. His eyes dipped to himself and he let out a curse Lam couldn't hear.

"What did you..."

His eyes rose back to hers, now colored with purples and reds. "You know, it's rude to stare." Even his accent was out of place, more contracted and casual.

"Oh, I'm so sorry, it's just... Your eyes..."

"They are wonderful." He gave a half smile.

Blushing, Lam looked down at her feet. This was one of her greatest annoyances, she could never control her blush, and it always seemed to come at the worst times. Humming, he ate one of the tarts in his hands and only then did Lam notice something—striped black and teal—swishing behind him.

"You have a tail!"

He turned around, his tail following. "Yes, it seems so." And with a flick, it was gone.

"You're the Cheshire Cat!" A smile twitched at the corner of Lam's mouth as her heartbeat doubled.

"Hats off to you" he said, taking off a top hat that had also been invisible on his head. "So now that you know my name, could I have yours?"

"Lamprocapnos."

His eyes lit up in curiosity. "Like the flower in the crest?" Lamprocapnos—bleeding hearts, to use its common name—were the flowers on the crest of Hearts. This crest was featured in the castle, uniforms, and armor.

"Exactly!" Lam blinked several times, making sure he wasn't an elaborate hallucination. "No one ever gets that."

"Have they never fought in a war?" he said with mock incredulity.

"Of course not. Anyway, you wouldn't need to be in a war to see it. Most people just don't care."

Cheshire gave an apologetic smile before his eyes grew lighter. "How old are you?"

"Sixteen." Resting a hand on the table, she moved back a step. "Why?" Up until then, she hadn't realized how close she was standing to him.

"So this will be your first Games." It was less of a question than a statement.

"Yes." Her heart sank.

He shifted back as if to get a better view of her face, his eyes moving through a different range of colors. "Are you scared?"

"Of course." Her voice was somewhere between her planned nonchalance and her true feelings.

Just then, the horns blew, and the Tweedles stepped up. The game directors were the only surviving members of Tweedle line, or...living person?

They were dressed in a red and black vest over a black shirt with two neck holes, one for each of their heads, and big puffy shorts over harlequin leggings.

"May all—" the right head's voice echoed over the entire hall from the top of the stairs.

"Of the contestants—" the left head was more quiet but carried just as well.

"Please make their way—"

"To the center—"

"Of the dance floor."

"Thank you."

Lam turned to say goodbye to Cheshire, but found he was walking right next to her, eyes forward and chin up.

"Are you going to compete?" Lam had never guessed he even *could* compete. But even as she asked it, she was reminded of a competitor from the year before... Then again, he seemed so opposite from the world of royals and aspiring nobles.

"Yes." His face regained some of its playfulness. "I'm tired of the lack of bread in this kingdom."

She couldn't help snorting a this. Although The Games were technically to determine whether the Board or the Deck got the farmland where the Looking Glass once swayed, it was far more about titles and entertainment.

His jaw was clenched and he stayed next to her all the way to the dance floor. She tried to not let her hands shake as she became the center of attention. Again, she was painfully aware of how short her skirt was; next to the other girls, she felt like she was wearing a bathing costume.

"Just remember you look like you."

Lam looked up to see the smiling face of Rudyard. He might not be the most caring brother all the time, but when she needed him, he was always there. "I see you found a friend. Cheshire." Rudyard nodded at Cheshire.

"Rudyard." Cheshire raised his eyebrows slightly. Then the trumpet blew for the second time.

"Find a partner—"

"From an opposing kingdom—"

"And let—"

"The dance—"

"Begin!"

CHAPTER

TWO

Lam was trembling so badly her crown began to slip, but she felt someone straighten it. She looked up to see her dance partner.

"Are you alright?" His hand fell from her head and brushed her arm as he took her hand and pulled her into his arms.

"Ah…" Her eyes slipped from his bright mock armor to his face. His light green eyes and his deep red lips were contrasted by pale skin and light blond hair. "Are you the son of a knight?"

He smiled in a slightly embarrassed way. "Actually, I am one of the White Knights."

Lam was shocked. "How old are you?"

"Seventeen and a half."

Lam's eyes grew wide. This boy was a knight? Not even a full man yet. How? How… Lam's thoughts were spinning faster than her body.

"I started to train when I was six," he said, as if he could read her mind.

"Really?" Lam let her feet fly, dancing in and out of the

center. Dancing had always been one of her strongest suits; she could move like no one else she knew, and even though she was small, she tended to start to lead. His eyes widened and he pulled her closer to his chest.

Air left her lungs as his arm pressed her back. People from Chess tended to dance closer and never lose eye contact; not at all how she danced. Her face reddened as she finally made eye contact.

"I'm Teon S. Wystan. What's your name?" He raised their arms and she spun underneath.

"Lam. Well, it's actually Lamprocapnos." Her heels made a bright ringing sound on the floor.

"So you're the princess?" His voice was deep and smooth, with the accent so particular to the White Kingdom.

She found it odd that he didn't know who she was. Being the center of attention had not been uncommon, especially with her male counterparts. "Yep."

His arm pulled her back after Lam's most recent spin. "What is it like?"

"It's wonderful!" Their feet once again darted close together. "I get to be so many things."

"What do you mean?"

She braced her hand on his biceps as he lifted her up. "Well, you see, I can be a mad student one minute and a sword fighter the next and then a lovely princess in puffy gowns and flowy dresses."

"I don't know about flowy, but it is puffy."

Lam felt self conscious, but there was nothing judgmental in his tone. When she looked down, he was smiling.

"Mine was also made by a Hatter." His hand caught her as she fell back into the final move.

"I knew it!" She was laughing, her face red from the exertion. "Only they could make something so strange."

"I'm glad you approve." Together with all the others, they rose, and then the dance was over. Lam found it to be short, but she would also have her last dance with him as was the tradition. But for now, she wanted to find Cheshire. He wasn't hard to find—again at the food table.

"Is eating your favorite hobby?"

"Dancing is quite the workout, especially when the pawn you're dancing with is overly excited... I feel like my arms are going to fall off." He stuffed an entire slice of pie into his mouth. He had his eyes on the food, but Lam knew he was watching her. "So how was your dance?"

"It was fascinating! Did you know that one of the White Knights is only seventeen!"

"Well, seventeen and a half." Cheshire reached for another slice of pie.

Lam felt a little disappointed. "How did you know that?"

"My secret." He turned, with a grin the width of his face.

"What even are you? What rank?" Lam said, studying him. She had the great fortune of being curious and the great misfortune of being quick to get in over her head. "Are you an ace? If so, which one? I've met the Ace of Hearts and—"

Cheshire was suddenly standing right next to her, breath tickling her ear.

"Joker."

Lam's eyes grew wide.

Joker. This *boy* was a joker, the highest rank in both kingdoms? This boy who looked no older than her was one of the most powerful people in all of Wonderland?! Lam tripped back. Cheshire had a bored look and a mustache of powdered sugar on his face. This was the grand protector and peace keeper of the Kingdoms of Cards?

Cheshire sighed, "You look like I just ate your slice of cake."

"I do not," Lam said, fixing her dress. "I was just surprised. Do you know who the other one is?"

"Of course, but that is for him to tell you."

Lam felt a spark of interest. "Is he here?"

"Oh, no. You would know if he was. Best not invite him anywhere with...people."

"Who—"

"Have you ever been on a chandelier?" Color slipped into his bronze skin and she could have sworn he bit the inside of his cheek.

"No. Why?"

He scarfed down the entire slice of pie, talking over his chewing. "Because it's fun."

Then he pressed one hand into the table and went invisible. His path was still clearly visible, breaking crackers and creating crumbs as he pushed himself higher. Lam stood, slack-jawed, as the curtains began to swing and bunch with the grip of hands before swishing free as he jumped from the wall. For a moment, Lam lost track of him. It seemed Cheshire had just leapt off the wall and was gone. Then the chandelier closest to the wall swayed slightly and Lam focused her attention on it.

From between tiny, shining light bulbs, the relaxed form of Cheshire slowly bled into reality, one arm hanging past the cage of glass and gold, the other propping his head up as he stared down at her with a self-satisfied grin.

In the space it took for Lam to blink, he disappeared again. Several beats came and went before the soft tread of boots sounded next to her. She twisted to see him grabbing another snack.

Lam couldn't help the smile creeping over her face. "That's amazing! How did you do that?"

Cheshire scarfed down the second piece of pie. "The

hard way." His eyes gleamed a strange mix of yellows, blues, and greens. "There's a much easier way if you want to try."

Lam opened her mouth and meant to shut it, but the words came out before she could. "Really? Could I?"

Grinning even wider, he grabbed her hand and pulled her over to the side wall.

"This is a terrible idea!" Lam felt her legs start to shake and her heart beating at an immense rate in her chest.

"It's easy." His free hand swooshed away the curtain that was hiding a staircase. "Just trust me."

"Trust the joker. Great." Lam grumbled, but even as she said it, she felt her face twitch up.

"Yes, trust the joker like you always do. And also, don't go saying that out loud."

Lam fell quiet. In a way, they were always trusting the jokers, especially with all the hardest tasks and quests. It was just...in all the stories, the joker was an adult, not a boy addicted to sweets.

Cheshire knocked on the polished wood of the railing. "Alright. Ready?"

Lam looked around. "What? No!" They had made it to the balcony closest to one of the smaller chandeliers. It was a dizzying drop to the dance floor. She could see Rudyard and her parents dancing down, down, below.

"How did you land your fall?"

"I didn't." Cheshire stared at her with his eyebrows raised for a beat before clarifying. "Cheshires can float, but only short distances off the ground. I fell most of the way and floated down the rest."

"That's—" Lam bit off her 'amazing' and instead said, "unfair. You have a nice, easy way to get down!"

"Do you really think I would let you fall?"

"No." The word was out in a spilt second and hung in the air between them.

His eyes flickered red and gold, the color seeping into something deeper around his pupils. "Good. Now, again, are you ready?"

Lam let a sour smile play on her lips. "No."

Cheshire turned to her, looking her up and down. "Hmm, yes, your dress might be problematic for you and that hat will have to go." His hands reached up and pulled off her crown. The crown disappeared and the joker now seemed to hold nothing but air.

"Did you just destroy it?" A mix of fascination and outrage filled her tone.

"No." He tossed the crown behind him where it reappeared on the floor. "Now that's dealt with," he crouched on the railing and held out a hand, "it's your turn." His eyes shifted to a bright red for half an instant, staining his face with something Lam could feel in her gut. "Trust me, Princess."

Lam clenched her fists to stop them shaking. "You say that quite a lot."

His head fell to one side, where his smile looked like a crescent moon. "Do you?"

Her heel made a high thudding as her leg bounced up and down. She was scared, but she did trust him. The whole of Cards trusted him, even if they didn't know who they were trusting.

Her eyes fell and her voice was small. "I guess so." She *had* only met him that night.

"Not exactly the vote of confidence I was hoping for. Now, hold out your arms."

"Alright, but—" then she realized what he was going to

do, "Oh no, no no no you are not throwing me." She would have stepped back if her bouncing legs had cooperated.

"I thought you said you trusted me."

"Yes and I *do*, but I don't trust *myself* to catch a chandelier!"

"Well, you better." And with that Cheshire grabbed Lam by the waist and, quite gently, tossed her onto the chandelier. It would have been very hard for Lam to fall from that swaying cage. Still, her hands shook on the gold and her eyes refused to open. Why was she so foolish? Why was she here? Her left eye opened a hair before both her eyes grew wide.

Have you ever reclined in a glass of champagne? Have you seen golden bubbles pop and dance around you? Have you ever floated over a sea of royals and lived, for a moment, like a ghost? Her breathing was still heavy but it was for a completely different reason.

A weight tilted the world. "And this is why I love being invisible," his tone was one Lam had never heard before—something between selfish and completely transparent, "...why I love being none of many."

Lam turned to see the Joker come into the visible spectrum. His eyes reflected all the stars of glass.

Her voice was now like that glass, golden and curious. "So you won't be found?"

"No, so I can get there in the first place." Cheshire fell back, resting on the frame.

No one was going to look at one of the chandeliers. No one saw that the one to the far right from the entrance swayed slightly. No one saw the two competitors in that world made of light. And why would they? Curiosity and thoughtfulness were fading traits in Wonderland.

Except for the soft sounds of their breathing, they stayed silent as they stilled over the swaying dancers. Lam's fingers buried between the bulbs and bands of gold and her eyes searched between shards of glass.

She was the first to break the silence. "Joker, I've been wondering, are you the Cheshire from the stories?"

"No, that's... Well..." He rose to one elbow and looked up as if to find the answer in the sparkling crystal. "We–Cheshires–don't have parents. One day, we start existing, but the Cheshire you're referring to is the closest thing I have to a father."

Lam thought she understood. But that would make him... "How old are you, truly?"

His grin returned and his eyes fell to her."Would you believe me if I told you the truth?"

"I hope so."

Purple and blue mixed in his eyes. "Eighteen."

Lam looked at him for a very long time before she sighed, "What happened to people having a childhood?"

"Oh, I did. More than you." He laid back down and put his hands behind his head. "This is probably the most excitement you've ever had. For me, this is just another day."

He was right. She had never broken any rules except for being in a room alone with Mack sometimes. But to go on a chandelier, and with a boy her parents didn't know, with no way to get down and a real chance of falling...

Her eyes again returned to the dancers. "I guess you're right."

A smile tugged at his lips. "I usually am! But not with you." He didn't move, his eyes drifted shut and only the smallest twitch in his jaw gave any impression he was awake.

"How so?"

"You believe things that shouldn't be possible."

Lam's view of the royals was broken by the glass, her shot of reality distorted. "Alice came from a world of impossibilities. And to her, this–" Lam gestured around them, "Wonderland–was an impossibility."

"True," Cheshire nodded, "and one of those is that it's time for the last dance already."

"What!" Lam looked at her pocket watch and squeaked. When she looked back, Cheshire was on the balcony with arms open.

"Just step over to me. I won't let you fall."

She gave a nod and then, before she could think, she had one foot on the balcony railing and the Joker had one of her hands. Gently, she set her beautiful shoes on the smooth floor.

If anyone noted the swaying chandelier, they didn't call out.

~

TEON SEEMED EVEN TALLER after spending time with Cheshire. "Have you enjoyed your night?"

"Oh yes, have you?" Her face was flushed and she didn't dare look up into his eyes.

"I suppose so. I didn't see you. Were you also dancing?"

"Well—" She couldn't say she had broken countless rules, and of course he didn't see her because she was fifty feet above him. "No, I was at the food table for a while and ran into one of my brother's... ah, friends." In fact, she wasn't even sure how well Rudyard knew Cheshire, but it seemed better than saying 'acquaintance.'

"Did you try the gooseberry pie? That came from my family's cooks." The pie that the joker had stuffed in his mouth had been gooseberry.

"No, but everyone seemed to like it." She felt her body fall in step with Teon's.

"I'm glad. That's the cook's pride and joy. What are your favorite desserts?"

"I love tarts."

Teon's face darkened. "Like—"

"The Evil Queen of Hearts? Yes." Her shoes kept the beat that his were having a harder time tracking. "But I will not have her ruining their name. Or mine."

His eyebrows ticked up and a muscle twitched in his cheek. "That's fair." He returned to leading the dance.

Teon's hand pressed into Lam's back and suddenly her chest was flush against him. His body was with hers—protecting, almost controlling her. Still, when she got over the initial surprise of being so close, she started to lead again.

Her face was almost teasing when she looked up and asked. "What is your favorite dessert?"

"Mmm...that's hard, but I do love pie."

"Gooseberry pie?"

He leaned in conspiratorially, so close she could feel his breath on her cheek and shoulder, his body curved around hers. "Don't tell the cooks, but my favorite is actually cherry."

Lam giggled as her heeled shoes pulled her back away from him for the final note. "Your secret is safe with me."

Soon it would be time to go, but she knew it was only the beginning.

The White Knight bowed, kissing her hand. "A pleasure as before, Lamprocapnos."

CHAPTER

THREE

"So, how did you enjoy your night?" Rudyard said with a smile.

Lam froze. What could she say? She could, maybe, tell him. But her parents, who were staring at her from the other side of the carriage, waited for an answer. She pretended to not have heard.

"Sorry, what?"

"The ball," Rudyard said with awful slowness, "How was your experience?"

"Oh, it was lovely. I danced with a White Knight, and I met one of the Cheshires. He was very nice. Didn't you think so?" Her voice was faster than she would have liked and it rose slightly.

Her father looked from the window to her with a surprised, almost worried air. "You met Cheshire?"

"There is more than one?" Lam's mother said at the same time.

"Yes." Rudyard loosened his tie as he spoke, "This one was in the last game. He won every round. Don't you remember the boy in the black cloak."

Both memories and an intake of breath filled Lam. Eyes, the eyes of a cat, looking up at her and... Her fingers twisted around one another as she fought to find something to say. "Also, he loves sweets. He spent all of his time at the food table."

The king half nodded, half frowned as he went back to staring out the foggy glass.

Rudyard's eyes narrowed. "Funny, I didn't see either of you there."

Their father's frown deepened and his eyes flicked back to Lam.

Her face started to heat. "Oh, well, you know that all Cheshires can turn invisible..."

"And so can the girl with the loudest crown in the whole room?" Rudyard pressed.

Lam's hand shot up to her bare head. Her crown! She'd completely forgotten it—lying, incriminatingly, on the balcony floor. "My crown..."

Rudyard began to clean his fingernails as he stared at her with pointed amusement. "Don't tell me you lost it."

"You lost your crown?" Their mother searched around, as if she could find it between the folds of her dress.

"Maybe she left it with her honesty? I was sure you had some this morning."

Lam felt the walls of the carriage start to close in. Having no other option, she glared at her brother in a very clear, *I-can't-tell-you-now-but-I-swear-if-you-pull-the-truth-from-me-you-shall-never-be-in-my-confidence-ever-again* look.

He gave a slow blink before sighing. "I think I saw it lying on the table. You probably took it off and forgot you left it there."

"Really? That was foolish."

Lam couldn't help internally cringing at being called foolish, even if she was. "I'll have to be more careful next time." Eager to change the subject, Lam looked down at her hands and the dress below them.

"Hatter made me a new dress!" The transition could have been smoother, but at least now her mother was staring at something else with a slight frown.

"Ah yes, that dress..." She ran one gilded finger over her lips. "Hatter should really check with me beforehand."

"You don't like it?" Lam said in a small voice.

"Goodness no, I love it! But still, it could be a bit longer."

"Very true," her Father echoed, "You must be careful what you wear."

"Yes Papa. I was smart about who I danced with."

"More like he kept you from falling," Rudyard said with a smirk.

Lam thought her face and neck must match her dress by now. "That's not true! And who were you dancing with?"

Rudyard stretched. "If you must know, it was the Princess of Red Chess."

Everyone gasped.

"How did it go?" Mother whispered, her eyes the size of roses.

"Well, she was almost half a foot taller than me and has a very imposing demeanor." His eyes drifted to stare out of the carriage window. "That is...until she started to laugh. Then she's just pretty." Rudyard had red on his ears and neck that was slowly invading the rest of his face.

"You made a member of the Red Court laugh..." Mother said in a dreamy sort of way. "My son. How?"

Rudyard winked, "Secrets of the trade."

This got a smile out of their father. Soon the ground changed, and they were back home.

Lam was so tired she forgot to clean her teeth and water

her bleeding hearts. The only thing she did was take off her clothes and put on her nightgown and fall into blissfully warm sheets.

~

"WHAT REALLY HAPPENED?"

Rudyard was standing over Lam when she woke up. Instead of answering, she pressed a pillow onto her face, only afterward remembering she still had her makeup on. With a groan, she went to the bathroom sink.

"Are you ever going to tell me where Cheshire took you?"

Lam caught Rudyard's reflection in the mirror. "What are you talking about?"

"Oh please, do you think I wouldn't know if my sister wasn't at the same table?"

"It's a big table, and also, I thought you were too lost in the wonder of a different princess."

Rudyard reddened slightly, but didn't take the bait. "Just tell me."

"Would you believe me if I told you the truth?"

"I hope it's not that bad."

"I was in a chandelier."

Rudyard was quiet long enough for Lam to finish washing her face. Her red eyes rose to meet their double in the mirror. Her most striking feature wasn't made with make-up, although it could easily be mistaken for such: black triangles, one going up the right side of her face, and the other one going down the left side, with hearts above her left eye and below her right. All members of any royal family in cards had some markings. She loved how bold hers were. Rudyard's were more subtle: hearts on the palms of his hands.

"So, you just met a Cheshire and went fifty feet in the air

with him...*alone?*" Rudyard said, shattering Lam's train of thought.

"You were the one who greeted him," she countered.

"He's a man you don't know." Leaning on the wall across from the sink, Rudyard muttered something else under his breath before saying, "What right does he have to compete anyway?"

Lam stopped in the act of drying her hands. What could she say? She couldn't just tell him...

"I know that look," Rudyard straightened, resting his hands on his hips. "It's the *I-must-keep-someone-else's-secret-but-don't-know-how* look."

"Even if you are right, it's none of your business."

"Actually, who my sister is spending time with is a part of my business."

"He's—"

"A joker," Cheshire said with a bow.

Both Lam and Rudyard stared at the now visible joker. He was in black from shoulders to toes, with gloves, long sleeves, slightly oversized pants, and black boots. Even his eyes were ringed in darkness, though it was a shade of tiredness. He toyed with the fingers of his right glove while he stared at Lam in the gold lined glass. His eyes slipped from her as he walked from her room to her bathroom. "I've never been in here..." Again his eyes flashed red, though now they were tipped with blue. "It suits you, Princess."

Suddenly Lam's view was blocked by Rudyard's back in the mirror. "How dare you sneak into my sister's room?"

Lam would never have considered Rudyard tall. He stood less than a head taller than her, but next to Cheshire he could almost be mistaken as such. She moved from the sink to stand beside the boys as they glared at one another.

"I didn't *sneak*. I would never *sneak* into her room." The joker's eyes had darkened and a muscle flinched in his nose. "I was let in."

"By the guards?"

"By the King."

Rudyard's face paled and his eyes flicked to Lam's. "Wait, did you say you're a joker?"

"Why yes, do you dislike jokers?" The Cheshire's voice was velvet, but now it was stretched out like hot taffy. He looked to Lam, tilted his head, and let his pointed teeth poke through his smile. "Your sister seemed to like me well enough."

Lam felt her face grow hot, as her body sparked all over. "It wasn't like that, and that's quite wrong of you to say."

A bemused, almost disappointed expression stole his smile. "I only meant you, at least, can believe in things that seem impossible. Your brother seems to need a demonstration."

Rudyard shifted to lean over Cheshire. "I would like to see that."

Somehow, the four inch height difference only made Cheshire seem greater and more imposing. "Excellent. I will be in the practice field. Come down when you're ready."

"You know this is my house, not yours." Rudyard said to the fading form of Cheshire. Only then did he realize that Lam was still in her nightgown. His face went red and without a word, he ran after Cheshire.

Lam was soon dressed and ready.

Both of the boys were there in full padding, which made Lam feel naked with just forearm protection.

"Should I..." Lam ran out of words.

The joker's gaze seemed to map her, from the sleek, dark red of her shirt, to the deep brown of her pants, then up to her face. "No," it was short, blunt, and brought a slight flush to his face, "you're fine." He started unclasping his armor and looked to Rudyard, who was doing the same.

With quick, mirrored movements, the joker unbuckled both sides of his chest guard. His movements were so perfect, Lam couldn't even guess which one was his dominant side. The padding fell to the ground and he moved to take of his shin guards. Everything about him was controlled and swift, from his hands to the small puffs of his breath, barely visible in the cold air.

"All right." Standing, the joker caught Lam staring and smirked. "Impatient?" He swept the padding from the ground and moved towards her. Lam began to step back before he walked past her and set the protection on the ground by the entrance tunnel. The joker moved to stand before both Lam and the now moving Rudyard. Cheshire rotated a wooden knife in his hands that had not been there a moment before. "Well, while your brother puts up his gear, d'you want to get started?"

"Yes, please." She, too, retrieved her mock knife from the sheath on her leg, albeit much less elegantly than him.

His hands rose as if to show her the knife, but it was impossible to follow as it rolled in, out, and around his fingers. "I'll be using wood, Is that ok?"

As often happened when she was about to spar, her mouth began to twitch into a smile. "I'm used to metal."

Cheshire's eyes followed this shift and his pupils dilated. "Good."

He came at Lam so fast she had to bend backwards to avoid his strike. His bearing was completely different, his eyes were wide and almost completely filled by pupils. The wood hit her again and again—sometimes lightly, almost gently, and others times it made her clench her teeth. He seemed unstoppable until, after five whole minutes, she sidestepped and for half an instant his left side was open. She took the chance right under his lowest rib. What was only a nick changed his whole demeanor. He straightened and started to laugh, his eyes returned to their old kaleidoscope of color.

"You amaze me more and more."

"Why?" her voice was tight and quiet from her lack of air, "You hit me at least a dozen times."

The joker's pupils shrank and his eyes shifted green. "Because I thought I would win flawlessly, like I have the last twenty-five times."

Lam's flush became a blush and she stepped back to watch as Rudyard had his turn.

Rudyard's knife control was better than Lam's, but the way he moved his body was stiff. Again the joker's eyes became black, but this time the rings of manic yellow were clearly visible. His knife shot up and slammed under Rudyard's chin before he twisted and sent his elbow into Rudyard's stomach. The wood blade was suddenly in his other hand and the first was grabbing Rudyard by the shoulder and flipping him over his back. Breathless, bruised, and more than a little angry, Rudyard could do nothing as the joker stepped on his wrist and stole his knife.

Spinning both knives around his hands, he stepped away from the prince. "One to none, Princeling." Green and blue eyes moved to Lam's, which were frozen on his hands. "I'll count my fight with you as another victory, if you don't mind."

Lam's wicked smile reappeared as she gripped her knife. "I do mind."

The boy flung his arms wide, stilling the blades in his hands—one wood, one steel. "You want to go again?"

A thrill went through her at having someone so impossibly better than her to fight. "Absolutely." This time it was her rushing at him.

Rudyard had mastered the art of sword play, but Lam had always been faster to try and win rather than play fair. Her metal skimmed the joker's cheek as her second hand grabbed his right wrist. His left hand, the hand with the wood, stabbed at her shoulder, making her right—and dominant—arm feel numb. Swiftly, he dropped the metal knife, slid from her grip, and grabbed it before it hit the ground. Then, the steel was to her throat and the wood had circled to the back of her neck.

"I win again." The words clouded the air.

Lam sighed and pulled back.

How was he so good? He seemed liquid, finding every crack and crashing against the defenses she tried to build.

Rudyard's hand fell onto her shoulder and he moved to take his blade back. Again he sparred and again he lost. They went around and around like that till midday and all three were tired.

The joker yawned, his face splitting open, before he looked up at the sky. "Well, I think you two should go see Hatter for your outfits."

Lam swiveled her head to look at him. "Our whats?"

"The clothes for the first game. It's at three o'clock, I think," Rudyard put in, still out of breath.

Lam no longer felt tired. "But I thought it was in the evening."

"In the past, yes." The joker stretched, pushing his back into the wall of the training ring. "This year, it's at three."

"But—"

"You'll do fine. The first game is always boring—something popular with the host kingdom or something," he sighed, "Too bad it's never in the Forest."

Lam blinked in surprise. The Forest? The Forest was outside the rule of both the Board and the Deck and was said to be more powerful than both of them combined...if its people could ever cooperate with one another. She had never really thought of it as a kingdom.

The Cheshire met her eyes. "It's not a proper kingdom, if that's what you're wondering." Shrugging one shoulder, he started to lead the way. "At least Hatter always has some sweets, even if they are usually stale."

Together, they went up to Hatter's quarters, which always smelled like tea and freshly ironed fabric. When Lam stepped from the spiraling stairs into the tower, Hatter shoved a bundle into her arms and pointed to the changing room. She opened the parcel to find puffy shorts with knee-high socks, a shirt with puffed sleeves, and her favorite pocket watch. It was everything she loved to wear on a fine spring day to play field games. When she came out, Rudyard was already dressed. He was wearing a ringmaster outfit, complete with long blazer and intricate vest and white bowtie. Then Hatter turned to Cheshire.

"And for you, I have two options. Joker or jester?"

"I'm sorry, what?"

"Which do you wish to go as?"

"But—"

"Just pick, and then we can have tea."

"Joker," the boy sighed, taking the bundle to the changing room as if being banished.

"Oh, Cheshire," Hatter fished in his pocket. "Hare told me to give this to you."

The joker looked back at the bottle of silvery liquid that

Hatter held up. Shifting the clothes to one arm, he grabbed the bottle. "Ah, thanks."

The man paused, still holding the bottom of the bottle. "Do you ever...regret it?"

The joker's eyes flicked over to Lam. Smiling, he looked back up at Hatter. "Not a day in my life."

CHAPTER

FOUR

By the time the joker came out, tea was ready and Rudyard and Lam had chosen cups. When she saw him, Lam choked on her tea. He was wearing a military captain's uniform in black and red with hints of cyan. A broken mask covered his eyes and a long black cape trailed over one shoulder.

Rudyard raised his eyebrows, side-eyeing Hatter. "And I thought you didn't pick favorites."

The joker gave him a teasing grin. "Just think of the outfits as a reflection of our skills."

"Then Lamprocapnos would be the most powerful," Mack said as he came in. His face lit up when he saw the Cheshire and he walked over to grab his head and ruffle the already messy curls. The joker grinned up at the much taller boy before pushing his hand off.

"Good to see you, Mack." Then his attention turned to Lam, his cape gliding out behind him. "Also, you have a point." His eyes found Lam and his mouth twitched again. She could feel the red invading her face, she could also feel that this was exactly what he wanted to see. Delicately, the princess raised her eyebrows, stared back, and drank the rest of her tea, waiting for him to give up. When he finally did, he wore the ghost of a smile. As her cup touched the table, words appeared on the bottom: *you have been poisoned.*

"Your pottery is as fine as your clothes, Hatter."

His eyes lifted as his head stayed bowed over one of the King's suit. "Thank you, but if your silent battle is over, I do believe it's time to leave."

Embarrassment dropped her confidence and her eyes back to the table as she reached for one last cookie.

"Are you joining us?" Rudyard asked, looking green. His cup also said *you have been poisoned, but* he did not share Lam's amusement.

"Only to the gates," Hatter replied, shooing away the tea pot. "Then you're on your own. I will be with the king and queen in the stands."

It was surprisingly easy for all of them to get into Hatter's tiny carriage. Sadly, the ride was not so easy. The whole time, Lam was painfully aware of Cheshire next to her and Rudyard's scowl wasn't helping. What entertained her for the two hours was the deck of cards that Mack always had on hand.

They played Quartet, of all things. Cheshire kept leaning over to look at her hand, forcing her to crowd into the corner. Even without seeing her cards, he kept saying things like, *'Hey, give me your kings,'* or, *'Would you be so kind as to hand over your aces?'* Each time taking at least two, if not three, cards.

"Oi, I want—"

"No!" Lam clutched her hand to her chest.

He smirked and reached over. "That's not how this game works."

"Go bully someone else!" She twisted her body so he

couldn't reach her hand. "You seem to know Mack well enough."

"I've known Mack for years, but he doesn't have what I need."

Rudyard turned his glare on Mack. "How do you know him?"

Mack blinked slowly, hiding his green-blue eyes for a moment. "I'm the son of the Head Advisor and the Advisor to the Prince and Princess. I meet people."

Rudyard grumbled something else, but didn't speak again as the joker held out his hand to Lam.

"My queens, if you'd please."

She scrunched up her nose as she held out her hand, the backs facing him. "They're all yours if you can find them."

Without missing a beat, he reached over and pulled her Queen of Diamonds, Spades, and Clovers from where they rested near the right side. Lam didn't even bother to stop her jaw from falling open.

"How did you just do that?"

Pulling the Queen of Hearts from his hand, he slapped the stack on the other cards resting by his side. "Wouldn't you like to know?"

Lam had never seen eyes so bright nor colors change so fast. In the end, to no one's surprise, the joker won with ten quartets.

At last, they arrived. It was odd to see all the same people from last night now as opponents. Curious faces were hidden behind hands as young nobles consorted with their friends and tried to discover what the first game would be. Squaring her shoulders, Lam walked into the crowd. She moved as if she was looking for someone or something, but she had nothing. All of them were in a waiting room of sorts, a tunnel that led to the playing field where the first game was to be held, hidden from them by thick vines.

"Are you lost?"

Lam spun around. There stood a girl around her age with large, round eyes like a nocturnal creature. Her eyes weren't the only thing that was strange—her skin was unusually yellow and see-through. She looked scared, but confident, like she was waiting for a blow she knew she could block.

"Well, are you?"

"To answer that, I would need to know where I am and where I'm going." Two things Lam herself would like to understand.

The girl nodded like Lam was a great teacher and friend. "Well, I found you, so you must have been looking for me."

Smiling, Lam held out a hand. "If so, then I would like to know who it is I found."

"My name is Myla Q. Babble," her fingers were cold on Lam's skin, "and who have I found?"

"Lamprocapnos S. Hearts, but most call me Lam."

"You are a brave girl," Myla said in a hushed tone. "Where is the boy who was also brave?"

"Who, my brother?"

Myla's fingers tightened on Lam's arm, and she shook her head. "The one whom you trusted."

The way that she said it made Lam blush. "Oh, you mean..." What should she call him? "He's somewhere."

"Somewhere can be very close if you're flustered."

It was just a whisper, but it made Lam want to scream. She spun around for the second time that afternoon, both times because of whispers. There stood the joker with a piece of cake, which made Lam remember that she had only had a few cookies that day.

"Where did you get that cake?"

"From the table, of course," he stepped in front of her, "but you can only have some if it's your unbirthday."

Lam huffed. "It *is* my unbirthday."

"Well then," he said, swooshing back his cloak, "the cake is all yours...if there's any left."

There was still cake. It was carrot cake, Lam's favorite. Biting down on her slice, she returned to Myla.

Between Myla's fingers, a cat's cradle formed. "He likes you."

"Irrelevant," Lam coughed around her last bite, "and unlikely. Where is it that you come from?"

Myla did not counter Lam's blatant change of subject. "I'm the Three of Clovers."

Lam shook her head. "I think the numbers shouldn't have to compete." This whole game had started when the Princes of Chess challenged the Princes of Cards to a battle of sport. The stupid boys kept it going until all of them were kings and could pass it on to their children. "This isn't your problem."

"But it's an honor."

"What do you mean?"

Myla's eyes drifted back to her hands and she pulled two of the strings and formed a star. "You have luxury. To you, this is a task. To us, it is a place to show our worth."

"But—" Lam's counter failed as she thought. All of the royals were at The Games, so it would be an excellent place to be seen and respected. "I guess..."

Just then, the Tweedles came in blowing their twin horns, saving Lam from her half-baked thoughts.

"Will all—"

"Of the contestants—"

"Please form—"

"A line."

Myla grabbed Lam's hand and pulled her to the front. "Here, we can play together. It will be fun!" They were the first two in line.

"How are you two?" Deevon, the left head, said with a smile.

"Good, how about you two?" Lam asked, even though the girls scared her a bit.

"Quite excellent, thank you," Day, the right head, replied with a nod. Today, they wore a blue and yellow dress, the color split down the middle. As they turned to lead them onto the field Lam could see a very large bow at the bottom of their back.

"Here we go!" Deevon began.

"The moment you've all been waiting for."

"Choose—"

"Your—"

"Flamingo!"

The vines pulled back to reveal a shining meadow, covered in little hills and tiny rivers, all gilded with a hundred bright arches.

Myla looked confused, but Lam was grinning ear to ear, wider than a Cheshire. It was croquet! She was a wizard at croquet.

"It's croquet." Lam started walking onto the field, the first to salute to her parents and the rest of the assembled royals. "I'm sure they'll explain the rules, but the gist is—"

The twin announcers spoke in their ringing voices, "The first game on this annual championship is—"

"Croquet!"

"The objective of the game—"

"Is to hit your ball—"

"To the end of the course first."

"It must go through—"

"Every single arch,—"

"Forwards and—"

"Backwards."

Deevon raised a finger. "If your ball is hit by another—"

Day raised her's as well. "You will be forced to start over."

"The first person to reach the end—"

"Will be the winner!"

"Best of luck to all!"

Lam leaned over towards Myla, "A long time ago, they had the cards bend backwards and be the arches, and used real flamingos and hedgehogs."

Myla, who'd also raised her hand in salute, kept her eyes, and worried expression, on Lam. "How awful."

"I know."

As they moved closer to the flamingo-shaped mallets, Lam half wondered if her father had planned this for her.

No royal was allowed to help a contestant, but there were no rules against the host kingdom assigning a game more common in their home. Just the year before, when the Games were hosted in the Kingdom of Red Chess, Rudyard had almost lost the first game for the simple fact he'd never done ring riding and no one explained the rules.

Looking behind her, Lam saw plenty of people appearing anywhere from confused to down right scared. Confidently, Lam reached in and pulled out a beautifully painted red and gold mallet. Myla tried to follow Lam's example, but she seemed to fear the wood would come alive and bite her hands. Eventually, she pulled out a black and brown bird before following Lam to the balls.

Each was intricately carved to look like a real hedgehog, with little patterns around the eyes and tiny paws curved into their bellies. Lam chose a rather small one that matched her flamingo—gold, with a heart on its stomach—before moving aside.

"It's a good day for it," Teon said, lifting a white and gray ball.

"Yes," Lam couldn't stop the excited flush filling her cheeks, "I can't wait."

"Good, because you're going first." Teon's smile was amused, making Lam flush even more.

Of course she would be going first. Who else would? Walking to the starting pole, Lam tried to hide her misgivings. She set her ball down, tightened her hold on the carved bird legs, and let the world focus. Everything unnecessary was blotted out, as if someone had run a brush through a still wet canvas. Suddenly, the stands didn't matter, the other contestants disappeared, and she couldn't even feel the cold gaze of the one person she avoided looking at. What she could see grew rosy, almost burning, bringing clarity to what she had to do. The beak of her bird hit the ball's back and the world returned to normal.

It was magic in motion.

The hedgehog shot through arch after arch and came to a stop sixteen arches away. When she turned around, Teon's eyes were wide.

"Remind me never to underestimate you again."

"Of course," Lam said with a sweeping bow.

"Um, is it my turn?" Myla looked like that blow had finally come, and she wasn't expecting it.

Lam touched her arm. "You'll do great." Leaning in, she whispered, "You're holding your mallet upside down."

Red in the face, Myla grabbed the legs of her flamingo, while Lam walked to the back of the line where, to her surprise, stood the joker. He casually swung his black and teal flamingo back and forth and tossed his green-blue hedgehog up and caught it. "Good to see you play your cards well."

"Good to see you not eating for a change."

He tried to look affronted, but his face had probably never expressed that emotion.

"Also," Lam continued, with her hand on her hip as she tapped her fake bird to her leg, "what were you doing in my room this morning?"

His face fell neutral, bordering annoyed. "Believe it or not, I was supposed to be there." His mouth closed and he tilted his head to one side. "Well, not in your room exactly, but I was supposed to get you."

Her gaze roved over him, taking in the tightness in his jaw and the way his pupils had sharpened. "Why?"

"To teach you to fight." His face twisted into an almost honest grin. "Why else would the king want a joker around his daughter?" Then his nose twitched and the false smile fell into a true sigh.

"Did you see?" Myla bounded up. "I got it through four arches!"

Lam turned to Myla and let her shoulders relax. "That's quite impressive! Don't you think so?"

Cheshire's eyes moved from Lam to Myla. "Yes, I've only ever gotten six at one in my whole life."

Once everyone had gone, they were spread out across the field. This was where one had to be careful. If someone else's hedgehog hit you, you'd be forced to start over. Many people succumbed to this and some used it to their advantage, such as the joker. He was having the most fun.

"And the boy with the blue hair—"

"Takes another prince down!"

He turned from the Tweedles to say to the rather distant Lam, "It's cyan, not blue."

"Whatever it is," Wesley, the Prince of Diamonds, punched Cheshire's arm as he walked back to the starting pole, "it knocked me back twenty arches."

"Next—" Day called over the already tired field.

"Adelyn W. Queenside."

The Princess of White Chess barely seemed to notice her name had been called. In fact, she had been sitting in the stands when the game started, as if she'd forgotten she was to compete at all. Casually stepping up to her white and purple ball, she hit it in the completely wrong direction to smack it into Lam's gold one.

"Oh—" Deevon sympathized.

"Now that was a tricky one." Day continued.

"Looks like—"

"The dear Princess of Hearts—"

"Will have to start over."

Adelyn gave a half smile as Lam picked up her ball and walked to the back of the line with Wesley. He had his flamingo resting over his shoulder and shook his head as she walked over.

"The downside of being the best out there."

Lam bore the ghost of a smile. "It was bound to happen." She knew Wesley mostly through Rudyard. The two princes were good friends despite the vague tension between the two kingdoms.

He nodded towards her brother, standing a little way away from the older Princess of Red Chess. "Two crowns he has a crush on her."

Setting down her ball, Lam let her smile become full. "I'm not betting against that."

He made a tisking sound. "Yeah, you and everyone else."

"Next—"

"Lamprocapnos S. Heart."

Her mind sharpened once more and she sent her ball through eighteen arches. She couldn't help tossing her head back as she stood and walked to stand near it. That was, until she saw Adelyn twirling her hair between her fingers as she looked at the joker with overly widened eyes. She was more than five inches taller than him, but still, he managed to seem imposing and charming.

She was saying something too distant for Lam to hear, but the Joker made an angry, almost disgusted, face. She could see him say the words *no thanks* before he walked away and caught Lam's eyes. Giving her an overly exaggerated eye roll he put his hand to the side of his head in a gesture Lam didn't recognize, but knew couldn't be a compliment.

Snorting, she flicked her eyes into a roll as well, which got a grin from the joker. As the Tweedles called for Myla, he moved closer to Lam, using his mallet like a cane. "Well, you're somehow still doing quite nicely."

"You're not doing too poorly, either."

His smirk was lopsided as his eyes turned from green to blue. "I've been doing it for years."

Lam leaned her flamingo on her leg. "I've been wondering about that. If you grew up in the Forest, how did you play croquet?"

"What, you think all of the Forest is uneven, craggy tree roots?"

"Well, no."

His smirk became teasing. "You don't *now*."

"And I never did." Her face was already starting to flush. As the red creeped into her face, it did the same in his eyes.

"You all know so little about it."

"Thats because no one ever comes from the Forest!"

"I came from the Forest."

"You're special."

He tilted his head. "Aw, thank you."

Lam wrinkled her nose. "You're welcome."

Something rolled towards them and the joker had to lift one foot to let the hedgehog roll under. It was only then than Lam realized three people had gone in the time they'd been talking and she hadn't been paying attention to anything that had happened. Her gaze flitted around to find everything pretty much the same.

"Worried?" The joker's words were too close and too low to be appropriate. "I know, I am rather distracting."

Lam glared at him from the corner of her eye. "No."

"No, you're not worried, or no, you don't find me distracting." He was standing a good two yards from her but by the way he spoke, his lips could have been pressed to her ear.

Lam opened her mouth, but Cheshire spoke first. "I won't take both as an answer."

"And I wasn't going to say both. I'm not in the fashion of lying."

His eyes closed slowly as he hummed low in his throat. "That's good." His eyes opened and Lam felt her throat close up. The joker stared at her with eyes so dilated they looked black. "I hate lies."

Something was pounding. It couldn't be her heart. It was all over her skin—touching her tongue and teeth and making it hard to breathe. It was far too intense to be natural. Perhaps it was another power Cheshires had. She had to look away. Her body was starting to spark with her lack of air and spots were appearing in her eyes. But none of them were as dark as his eyes or as deep as the ring of red that surrounded the darkness.

The red was interrupted and in an instant it all became purple, and his pupils shrank. He made a face as if there was something acidic in his mouth. It was a look Lam didn't see as she closed her eyes and turned away. Her heart—for that was clearly what it was—beat even harder for a moment. It was all wrong in the way it beat—hard then absent, as if she was losing it and feeling it for the first time all at once. Snapping her eyes back on the game, Lam watched as her brother hit his hedgehog through three arches and clapped with everyone else as it came to a comfortable stop halfway to the pole.

"Next—"

~

It was another hour and a half before Lam crossed the finish line.

Once the first contestant won, everyone only had five more hits. No one finished in their first or their second shot. Four completed in their third, sixteen got it in their fourth, and twenty-six in their last shot. For a moment, Lam was excited. Her brother was walking over to her with a grin, her parents were cheering from the stands, and the sun seemed to smile as it started to fall towards the soil. Then the realty of it all shot into her. Looking up at the scoreboard, she saw her name in the largest letters right on the top where everyone could see it.

FIVE

Her eyes blurred as she looked up to her parents. They were both on their feet, cheering for her. But all to quickly, her eyes slipped to the other kings and queens. The King of Clovers, the current High King, was staring down at her with an unreadable expression, eyes hooded by thick brows, pulled low. Lam's eyes darted to where his wife, the Queen of Clovers, sat with her younger son, smiling at the older, competing son down on the field.

The Kings and Queens of Diamonds and Spades were also looking at their children, though their smiles were less broad, and the King of Spades had no expression at all.

A chill covered Lam's body as she turned to the royal stand of Chess.

He was staring at her, a smile on his lips and his head propped on one hand. When her eyes met his, his smile grew and he even went so far as to give her a little wave. Fear and disgust mixed in Lam's chest, but she couldn't look away from the Prince of White Chess. His lips parted and she knew what he was going to say, knew how his hand had brushed hers the first time he'd said it. Blood pounded in her ears, but she couldn't look away as his lips moved to mouth the thing Lam dreaded to be named.

'*Well played...*'

She didn't want to see his pale lips say it. Her whole body shook and tears rose to her eyes. She was going to collapse under her hate, going to cry at her own victory, going to fall to pieces right there...

"I knew you could do it!" Rudyard clapped her on the back, and feeling flooded into Lam as her eyes fell from the prince's last word. "You really set a new record and won your first game!"

"New record?" Lam felt blooderflies erupt in her stomach, but it was better than the cold she'd felt before. "What do you mean?"

"Just what I say," Rudyard pointed to the scoreboard. There, in golden letters, was '*New record for course!*' "That's something you don't see every day!"

Her father had held the old record. And now, here stood a little girl, a new competitor, a threat, who wished nothing more than to turn invisible.

"You know," a voice like velvet—soft, yet jagged—spoke behind her, "you can use this."

"Joker, will you stop sneaking up behind me?" Wearily, Lam forced her arm to raise in the customary salute.

He appeared in front of her and clicked his tongue. "You really need to stop trusting your eyes so much." His smile fell, and he became slightly more serious. "What I was saying was, now they fear you. Use that."

Turning away, she moved towards the tunnel. "But how? I'm not like you. I not some mystical creature who happens to be a joker. I can't convince people to do stuff." They walked together to where the adults and elders stood to congratulate them. Lam noted that Rudyard was talking to the Princess of Red Chess. Both were laughing quite a lot.

"You could if you were bold."

Lam raised her chin and stared straight ahead. "Bold. How many times have I heard that word describe me?" Lam's eyes turned to the Cheshire's and she stared as his eyes became red and blue. "Sometimes I do underestimate myself," she felt a smile rise from her chest, "but I would never say that I am not bold."

"Boldness is found in the heart," Myla said, coming from behind, "I guess that's why you have twice the rest of us."

Lam jumped. The joker's eyes widened and then looked back at the princess. He smiled and his eyes again shifted hue. "But then a thief would be the boldest of all."

Myla paused before nodding, "That is wise. Maybe it is the becoming that makes you bold."

And with that, they were in a crowd of people ready to congratulate the ones who passed and sympathize with the ones that lost.

"Oh my sweet girl, you were brilliant!" Lam's Mother smoothed down her curls.

"We are both so proud! And to beat my record?!" Her father's tears glistened in his eyes as he smiled down at her.

The queen tapped her lip with one of her fingers. "You could become an ace with a score like that!"

This made Lam pause. An ace? She had always lived in a strange paradox of growing up a princess, but knowing she would never rule. Did she want to be an ace? Had she wanted to be a ruler?

But then the image of what she wanted came to her.

Her eyes slipped from her parents to a memory: a blade darting under and over fingers, while a smile revealed sharp teeth. "But I want to be a joker."

The queen's tears stopped, and she held Lam at arms length to see her face. "A joker? But why in Wonderland would want to become that?"

"Because..." Lam was pressed back into the present. "They're the strongest, the best." As often happened, a smile began to paint her face. "No one can beat a joker."

Yes, that was it, she wanted to be seen for her strengths, wanted the be able to strike first, lose last. Lam wanted to...be safe.

But those words didn't come, so instead she turned her gaze to her mother and said, "They don't fear anyone."

The tears had come back into her mother's eyes, not of joy, but of a brave sort of sadness. "You are the only one who can choose your fate." Then her face took on a new intensity. "But you are choosing, not making. There are only so many paths. Remember that."

Lam nodded and hugged her mother again.

This was true. Many people had seen where their path led, but no one ever changed it—only the Storytellers had that power and only Wonderland knew where they lived. Her mother hugged her one last time and then went to congratulate Rudyard.

"We *are afraid*..." the joker materialized in the tree above her, his eyes were distant and black, "it's just not the sort of thing that we're known for."

Lam craned her neck to see him, feeling more than a little shamed. "Well, when I'm a joker, I won't be. Also, don't you have family to congratulate you?"

"Actually," swinging from the tree, he cupped his mouth with one hand, "I don't think that old Cheshire knows I'm here."

"Why? Doesn't he want to know where you are?"

The boy shrugged. "Maybe, but he spends most of his

time with Shire, the youngest Cheshire. To him, I've been fully grown for two years and he doesn't need to keep me out of trouble."

"Well, if he did, he would be failing quite miserably." Lam looked around at all the families showering their children with love.

"I think, in a way, he thinks it's a Cheshire's job to make trouble."

Lam looked back and smiled. "Then you should get a promotion."

Eyebrows rising, the joker took a step back. "But I haven't even painted all of your flowers!"

"All of them? That's a lot of work."

He puffed out his chest and cleaned under his fingernails. "And I'm a hard working man."

"Boy," Myla corrected walking away from her mother, father, and little brother. The Cheshire deflated. Lam smirked.

Hand on hip, he said, "Has anyone told you you have terrible timing?"

Myla tilted her head to one side. "Maybe it's just that your watch is wrong."

Lam knew she was going to be good friends with Myla. "Myla, save me! I'm afraid that the...he will drive me mad!"

"Oh, don't let anyone drive you mad. The walk is good for you." Myla patted Lam on the head, ignoring her stutter.

The joker turned red and brown eyes to Lam. "She's right, but if you want me to, it wouldn't be the first time I've taken someone there."

Lam glared at him, Myla still patting her head. "I'll take the walk."

"It will most likely become a run if you spend your time with Cheshire." A boy emerged from the crowd. He was in black and gold, a long trench coat over a simple white shirt and black pants. On his hands were an assortment of rings, no two the same. On his face, around his eyes like dark circles, he had black spades, the mark he was in that royal family.

"Missed you too, Ravenel." The joker leaned toward Lam. "He's just salty because the last time we sparred, he lost quite miserably."

Her eyes got even wider as she tilted towards Cheshire and hissed, "That's Ravenel F. Spade, almost the Crown Prince of Spades!" She didn't bother mentioning that Ravenel was the only royal from Cards to have won The Games in the last ten years.

The joker waved his hand. "Yes, he's quite disappointing. Here, we don't have to talk with him." Then he laced his arm with hers and started to steer her away.

"Wait, no—"

She expected Ravenel to be looking at her, but instead, he only glared at the back of the cyan head. Finally, his eyes fell to her. They were as cold and deep, as always. "Save it for The Games." And with a swish of his trench cloak, he melted back into the crowd.

"You two seem popular," Myla said from the tree that the joker had been in.

He smiled up at her. "It's because of my natural charm."

Lam huffed. "If insulting people falls under 'charm,' then yes."

"Of course it does, I charm them away." He waved his fingers in the direction of Ravenel.

Both girls laughed at that. From somewhere in his cape, the joker pulled out a taffy.

"What is wrong with you?" Lam's amusement shifted to baffled annoyance. "Why are you always eating sweets?"

He looked like she had just slapped him in the face.

"What? Do you expect me to eat savory food?" His lip curled at the word 'savory.'

"Oh look, it's Aldwin!" Myla said, waving her hand above her head. "Over here, Aldwin!"

A boy, or more correctly, a young man, in a brown leather jacket covered in key holes, a white shirt, and simple black pants walked over.

"It's so good to see you," he said, helping Myla down, "I saw your first shot. That was amazing!" He towered over Myla. Well, he towered over all of them. "Hey Cheshire," he nodded at the joker and then looked at Lam, "Good to see you again, Princess"

He held out his arm and his sleeve fell open revealing his markings—clovers, end over end, stretched up his arm.

Lam grabbed his hand and grinned up at him. "Same to you, Prince." It had been a long standing joke between them that they could never remember the other's name. For a long time, it was not a joke.

Lam turned to the joker, who just stared at her hand in Aldwin's with a glazed frown, and asked, "How do you know this guy?"

Aldwin chuckled. "Everyone knows Cheshire."

Lam sighed and turned back, letting her hand fall. "I'm starting to believe you're right." Her eyes scanned the crowd of people and this time they caught on something she'd rather not see.

Standing in a blank space, the Queen of Red Chess was surreptitiously scolding her daughters. One hand wrapped around the youngest's arm. The girls both stood in a willing kind of pain, like martyrs walking to the gallows. Shivering, Lam shifted to look away, only to see the other royal family of Chess. The prince was winding his finger through his sister's curls, catching them, holding them. The girl's back was to

Lam and the prince was half turned away, but Lam could clearly see the King and Queen of White Chess.

She'd heard stories about the White King's unnerving smile, but to really take it in was a completely different thing. The queen's face was no more settling, with her crown a gold band that circled over her eyes. Forcing herself to look away, Lam turned right into the prince's waiting gaze. He was a different kind of disturbing. His hand tightened through his sister's curls and his eyes shown with something between malice and delight as he stared down Lam.

This was why she never wanted to become a queen. Even the idea of having to deal with him made her feel sick. He was sick, every inch of him was, every piece, but somehow...no one else saw.

Blinking so hard her eyes started to water, Lam looked back at the joker. Or she would have, if he had been there. She looked to both sides and then up at the tree. "Where is—?" Lam stumbled, trying not to say 'the joker.'

Myla, who had again climbed the tree, looked down. "Hmm?"

"Where's—" Lam waved her hand in the vague image of the joker.

Myla pointed at something blocked by people. "He's fighting Ravenel over there."

"What?!" Lam pushed through the crowd to see Cheshire and Ravenel, both with knives drawn. "What in Wonderland!"

The joker shrugged, "Ask the knave."

And with that, they were on each other, going so fast that she could only tell them apart because of the cyan hair. After a little while, she was able to see them more clearly. This was because of her training, not them slowing down. If anything, they were getting faster. She didn't even realize that she was twisting her shirt until Rudyard rested his hand on her arm. When it seemed that both of them must collapse, the joker cut deeply into Ravenel's arm. With a yell, Ravenel fell to one knee. The Cheshire grabbed his hair and turned Ravenel's face up, clicking his tongue.

"I told you last time, don't pick fights you can't win." He was cut up too, but not even close to how badly Ravenel was.

The prince's clothes were in tatters and his face was covered in nicks, but he tore his head from the joker's hand and spat on his shoe.

Turning, the joker spoke to the crowd at large, "Someone call for the nurseturtiums."

"What about you?" someone called.

But the joker merely faded invisible.

"You must find a weapon that suits you." The joker gestured at the supply rack.

It was the morning after the first game and it was just the two them in the practice yard. Lam felt like she was breaking more than one of her parents' rules by being there. She crossed her arms, trying to not think how they could look from a window and see Lam standing two feet from a boy they hadn't met. "So, what's your weapon?"

The joker smiled in a way that made Lam's blood run fast and cold. He held out his hand. Resting on his palm was a small cylinder. He threw it into the air, twisted, and caught it in his other hand, but now it was a double sided sword-like weapon with a handle in the center. It was at least five feet long with a pearlescent sheen that reminded Lam of his eyes. Only then did she remember what they were discussing.

"That? That's your weapon?" Her eyes were the size and shape of Myla's. "How can you use that thing?"

He raised the weapon and closed his eyes. He was inside of a tornado of chaos, but he was serene. He was fully aware of his surroundings, never hitting any of the practice dummies, or her for that matter. He had full control over the weapon that was almost the same size as him. When he finally came to a stop, she realized she'd been holding her breath.

"How..."

He looked up. His face was back to normal. "Time, that's how." Then he waved at the rack, "Now it's your turn."

"But I can't do that!" Lam felt her leg shake.

"And no one is expecting you to, but first you have to find your weapon."

"You're saying it like it's magic."

The joker nodded. "It is magic—the magic of weapons."

And so they began. They tried everything. They tried long swords, short swords, two bladed swords, maces, ring swords, spears, staffs, and even a slingshot.

But then Lam remembered. When she was little, she and Rudyard would play with all sorts of fake weapons that their father had made to fit their tiny hands. When they were too big, they moved on to more common weapons.

"I want to try a battle axe." She raised her chin, ready to be told that was ridiculous. No fine lady fought with such a barbaric weapon. But when she met his eyes, he looked curious, not judgmental. Without a word, he went to find a battle axe.

As soon as she felt the cool grip, Lam knew it was the one. For the first time, she felt the magic he'd talked about. She resonated with the cold, deadly object in her hands. It was beautiful, even graceful, with a black handle and a red blade—the heart hollows made even more striking by the gold ridges. She began to dance in the same pattern that Cheshire had, albeit a lot slower.

"I think you found your weapon." Grimacing, he looked off into the misty distance. "Sadly, I know someone who uses a battle axe."

"Why is that a bad thing?" She asked, tossing her axe from hand to hand.

"Because it's the other joker."

Lam's heart quickened and the corner of her mouth quirked. "Will I finally meet him?"

This joker looked at her, amused. "If you think you've waited a long time, you don't know him." The boy sighed. "But we will have time before the next game, and I should go see Cheshire and Shire."

"Are they on the way?"

"Yes. It takes around five hours to get there by carriage and we have two days til the next game, so..."

But Lam was already on her way to tell Rudyard and go pack.

"YOU MUST BE SAFE, you hear me?" Lam's mother squeezed her arms, her deep red hair gilded by the setting sun. "I'm not sure if I trust that Cheshire boy, and to go see a joker..." The queen shuddered.

Lam was so close to telling her *that Cheshire boy* was also a joker, but she bit her tongue. After the footmen put their luggage on the top of Hatter's carriage, it was time to leave. Only Hatter, Mack, Lam, Rudyard, and the joker were going. There was a train that ran from Hearts to Diamonds, but it was slower and ended in the capital, so they would have to either walk or use a Diamonion carriage.

After the first few hours, and passing completely through Diamonds, they entered the Forest. As they passed over the moss covered bridge to the land beyond Cards, Lam started to trace the path, trying to take in every tree and stone in the hope that she could map it in her mind.

The joker's eyes drifted open, and he blinked himself from his meditation. Leaning forwards, he looked out the window with her, their breath fogging the glass. "You can't find your way back from this point on unless you don't want to."

Lam raised one eyebrow. "Then how does Hatter know?"

He leaned back, taking up more than the allotted quarter. "The magic only works if you're going back, and also, he's mad. This magic can't work on someone who's mad. So all of us could get back except for you and Lord Stubborn over there." He nodded at Rudyard.

Rudyard stirred in his sleep but did not move from where Cheshire had crushed him in the corner. Mack, too, was asleep, his legs tucked close to his chest, not even touching her with his toes. Her eyes moved to the joker, and he stared back, the color of his eyes barely visible in the light from the moon and stars.

"You don't have to sleep." Shifting, he turned his face back to the window. "I personally hate sleeping." There was something dark and playful in his tone.

"Why is that?"

His jaw clenched and his eyes widened for a moment.

Quickly, Lam back-peddled. "You don't have to tell me if you're not comfortable saying."

Chuckling, he shook his head and closed his eyes. "I just have nightmares." Eyes opening, his lips parted and he intentionally fogged the window. Again, he glanced at her with red and green, then yellow and blue, then a mix of all four colors. "If you want to sleep, you have to stop telling yourself to sleep. Just let your mind go wherever it wants to, and soon we'll be there."

"I doubt that will work."

"Well, if it doesn't, I can just hypnotize you." The joker grinned, showing his pointed teeth.

"Can you really?"

He shrugged. "Never tried."

Looking up, she watched the stars though the glass top. "I guess I'll trust you on this one, too." Her eyes drifted shut and the last thing she saw was his smile, teeth shining in the moonlight.

"You always can."

Lam wanted to reflect on those words, but she was already bouncing around her thoughts, each was a trampoline that propelled her to the next one. Closing her eyes, she fell into it, letting the dream carry her. It took her to lots of places—to the past, the future, her mind, and finally to her whole body.

When she opened her eyes, the joker stood holding the door for her.

"See, what did I tell you?"

She could tell from the light of the setting moon that his eyes were rimmed with just a hint of red.

Rubbing her face, she realized her eyes had dreams. She went to brush them away but the joker's mouth dropped open.

"You would waste perfectly good dreams like that?" With one hand, he grabbed an empty glass flask from his pocket, and with the other, brushed her dreams into it. His fingers were warm and slightly calloused, laced with tiny cuts only the sensitive skin of her face could feel.

Often, Hatter had told her to collect her dreams, but she'd never had the patience. She had dreams every night. What made any of them worth saving? But, for the first time, as she stared into the joker's shifting eyes, she realized Hatter might have had a point. She wanted to know what kind of dreams he'd had. What stars of his imagination had been caught by his lashes? His fingers fell from her face and the joker set the glass vial in his cloak. Stepping out, he opened his arms, breaking the moment.

"Welcome to my home."

SIX

The joker held Lam's hand as she got out of the carriage. "What do you think?"

She blinked, not sure if it was from the fact that she had just woken up, or the magic of the Forest, or the low light, but all of the trees had faces. Her gaze moved to Mack and Rudyard, who were also blinking awake. Looking up, she found the joker, appearing apprehensive.

"It's beautiful."

He brightened.

She wasn't lying. It was the most beautiful place she had ever been. All of the colors seemed more real and yet shifting, like a gentler version of his eyes.

"It's beautiful," Lam repeated.

Walking over to one of the trees, Hatter rapped on its nose. "I'm sorry to disturb you Mister Willow, but we need to see Cheshire. Cheshire is back."

Lam looked to the joker as if that would make the statement any more clear.

Mister Willow opened his eyes slowly. "Ahhh, yes, is that scoundrel back?" He forced himself to find the joker. "Yes,

Cheshire has been expecting you. He could really use your help. Shire has been a nightmare to take care of."

The joker smiled and rose a little off the ground, in a dreamy sort of way. "Well, he is a Cheshire," he said, resting back down on the ground, "and Cheshire is teaching him."

Lam's brain felt like a watch that ticked without the hands moving. Her eyes opening and closing every time someone said 'Cheshire' as she tried to follow the conversation.

"Speaking of that..." Mister Willow glared at the joker, "Why don't you ever come back from time to time?"

He looked up in thought.

"It's been six months. Not one word."

Shrugging, he returned his eyes to the tree. "Been busy. Did they really miss me?"

"Of course we did, now come up here. Soup's almost ready," a voice remarkably like the joker's came from the trees.

Mister Willow sighed, "I guess you will have to use me." A ladder appeared on his side. He pretended to wince in pain, but didn't complain when, one by one, Mack, Rudyard, and Hatter went up.

"You might have figured this out, but I'm not a fan of heights," Lam said, knees knocking together.

"Don't worry, it's even easier than climbing onto a chandelier," the joker said with a smirk.

Rudyard turned at this, his eyes narrowing and looking down at Lam.

"...I'll be right below you."

Letting out a breath, she walked towards the tree and started to climb. When she made it to the top and looked down, she feared she was going to vomit.

"It's okay." The joker used a tone that she had never heard.

With one hand on her back, he led her over to the kitchen. Inside, on their left, was a stove and on their right was a table. By the stove, stood a man in his mid-twenties. He had bright silver hair—cut in the same style as the joker—and messy clothes that were a little big on his skinny frame. He looked almost exactly like the joker...except older. When this new Cheshire turned around, instead of the kaleidoscope of color that Lam was used to, he had purple, swirling eyes. He was smiling in a way that made it seem like he hadn't slept in a very long time.

"Good, Cheshire, you stir the pot, and you," he waved a Lam, "grab the spoons."

Looking around, she realized that everyone had a job, even a little boy no older than seven. With orange hair, striped skin like a tabby cat's, and a big smile, he moved around the kitchen, showing everyone where the various things were. When he saw the joker, he ran over, flinging both his arms around his older brother's waist.

"You're home!"

The joker laughed and held Shire's head. "Missed you too, Shire. I'll give you a real hug once the soup's off the heat."

Shire turned to Lam and bounced over to her. "Hello!" He grabbed one of her hands with his and pulled her to the silverware drawer, where, together, they grabbed the spoons.

Once the table was set and the soup off the heat, Cheshire picked up Shire.

After choosing a bowl, Lam moved to stand next to the joker. "Your naming system is awful."

He grinned and ladled a generous serving of orange soup for her. "Well, you don't call me by my name anyway, so it's fine, right?"

Shire looked up from the ladle, confused.

"Most certainly, Joker." Lam's gaze went from the joker's to the quizzical gaze of the old Cheshire.

Slowly, his eyebrows lifted and a smile spread over his teeth. Ducking her head, Lam moved from whatever thoughts he was forming in his mind as she went to sit down. When her face and the soup had cooled down, Lam took a sip. The flavor was sweet, not savory, but it was still one of the best soups she'd ever had. She tried not to inhale it, but she couldn't stop eating.

"So," Hatter said, leaning back, "is ah...the other joker coming by soon."

Lam was sure that he was about to say a name.

The old Cheshire looked up. "He has planned on coming for tea tomorrow in the morning."

"Excellent," the present joker said, leaning back.

"Excellent," Shire echoed sleepily.

"It's past your bedtime, little Cheshire," Old Cheshire said, "Cheshire, will you put him to bed?"

"Sure. Come on, Shire." He picked Shire up with surprising ease and walked out onto one of the bridges, slowly fading from view. Two people cleared their throats at the same time. When she turned around, both the old Cheshire and Rudyard were giving her pointed looks.

Lam tried to stop her skin from reddening by diverting the focus. "So...how long has the joker been living on his own?"

"Two and a half years, though I wouldn't strictly say he was alone," the old Cheshire said, his spinning eyes slowing.

"What—"

"More importantly," his eyes stopped moving all together, "how long have you known him and how long are you going to make him suffer?"

Lam felt a shudder run through her. "I—"

Coughing, Hatter leaned forwards. "Cheshire, she doesn't know…"

Lam turned to Rudyard, but he looked as confused as her. Shifting her focus to Mack, she found him staring at his father with careful blankness.

"How doesn't she know?" The old Cheshire's eyes had began to spin again. Tsking, he looked back at his soup. "Storytellers, I forgot." His next words were too muttered to hear, but Lam caught what she thought could be 'humans' as the joker returned.

"She'll give it when she wants to." The joker's eyes were black and purple as he moved into the kitchen. Shivering, Lam opened her mouth but he turned away as soon as she did. His eyes were hard as he looked at the old Cheshire. "She doesn't need to know."

"What don't I need to know?" The tension in the room had risen exponentially and Lam felt her hands began to sweat. "If it's something you need, I can give it to you." She started to run down a list of all her possessions. She had gold, and silks, and dresses, and money, but nothing she thought a joker would need. She had weapons, but he seemed able to access all the weapon stores in the castle.

"It's fine," the joker's voice cut through her thoughts like a knife, leaving the room ghostly silent.

Waving his hand, the old Cheshire filled the cold emptiness, "I'm sure you all wish to lay down. You can pick any of the empty rooms. We have enough to house a small army."

The joker started to go, too, but then Old Cheshire grabbed him by the shirt.

"Not so fast. You still have a kitchen to clean."

The joker's shoulders sagged, but he did as he was told.

Lam found it less scary to move about in the dark. The

ground could as easily be five feet below her instead of thirty. Still, the swaying bridges between trees made her legs feel like pudding, and the fixed walkways were even worse, seeing as they didn't have railings. She kept her exploring to only the closest rooms, though no matter where she went, she could find another bridge leading farther out. Old Cheshire hadn't been lying when he said they could host an army here, though its location couldn't have been worse for military escapades.

The room that Lam eventually chose was not the biggest, but it had the most character. The ceiling was tall, made with branches woven together and a smooth floor. The bed was only a little skinnier than her bed and it was a little longer. Next to the bed there was a lamp letting off a soft glow that made Lam drowsy. She changed quickly and then slid into the soft, fluffy sheets.

Her mind buzzed with questions. The joker seemed uncomfortable with whatever he needed from her, but she couldn't help but want to know...

Was he sick? Did she have some sort of medicine she didn't know about? Was he a sort of blood-drinking Forest creature from the stories? Was he cursed to only drink from one person? Or did it have to do with something she knew? Did she have a piece of information vital to his current mission? And how was she supposed to give it to him if she didn't even know what it was?

Her eyes began to drift closed, but it was a long time before she fell asleep and even her dreams were riddled with questions.

~

"It technically wasn't taken."

"But it's my room!"

"Well what do you want to do? We can't just move her. She'll wake up soon anyway; just let her stay."

Sun was streaming in through the leaves, letting gold and green light in as Lam opened her eyes. She tried to focus on the three people standing over her. They were all...vaguely similar. The Joker looked exhausted, Old Cheshire looked amused, and Shire looked confused.

"What are you doing in Cheshire's room?"

Moving to rub her eyes, Lam paused and blinked through her fogged brain. "I'm not sure... you, Cheshire...er, Old Cheshire, said to pick a room and no one seemed to use this room, so..." She tried to focus on the joker, "is this your room?"

He shrugged and ran a hand through his already mussed hair. "It was."

"Why are you only going to bed now?"

"Because," he glared at Old Cheshire, "I had some chores to catch up on."

"That's not my fault."

"Do you want some breakfast?" Shire asked, stopping a standoff between the other Cheshires.

"Once I get dressed."

Old Cheshire nodded and left with Shire following. The joker leaned over and brushed her dreams into a new flask. Again, her mind started mapping his finger tips, but she forced her thoughts away from his touch. Instead, rolling her eyes up, she mentally told him to not poke her in the eye. To her surprise, the small pieces of her mental state fell into the jar without her noticing.

"They weren't any good last night."

He paused, flicking slightly over to her eyes. "Were they nightmares?"

"No." Lam blinked as he pulled his hand away.

He nodded and set the flask into his pocket. When Lam was alone, she got dressed and as ready as she could be in a strange place about to meet a joker.

That day's breakfast was oatmeal. By the time she sat down, the syrup was gone and the brown sugar jar half empty. The only reason it wasn't all gone was that old Cheshire was floating, the jar in his hands, and both young Cheshires were too short to reach.

"We're saving it for our guests. Now sit down."

Both of them fell into their seats with a huff. The joker gave a sorrowful look at his oatmeal that was at least sixty percent sugar.

Lam smiled and took a heaping spoonful of the sugar. "So, when is tea time?"

"All the time," the voice was soft and scratchy, but it would command armies if it wanted to.

Lam felt all her hair rise. She would have screamed except she was too frozen to make a sound.

"But I'm here now, if that's what you're asking."

SEVEN

L am spun around to see the other great protector and peace keeper. He sat with his legs crossed and resting on the table. He held a vaguely humanoid shape and size, though taller than most, but he could never be mistaken as human. He was clothed in a brown coat over a stained shirt and dark brown pants. The coat had mismatched buttons going all the way up the hood. In his right hand, he held three pocket watches, and in his left hand, he held a teacup that was laced with cracks. Even his eyes were mismatched, one big and brown the other liquid gold. As she watched, it started to drip down his face, its path impaired by the fur that covered the male's entire body. Her gaze lifted to the large brown rabbit's ears poking from his hood. They were as disheveled as the rest of him.

"You know, it's rude to stare."

Lam flinched, reminded of the joker—Cheshire—and how he had greeted her the same way. The new joker's face broke into a smile.

"I heard that you use the battle axe." The gold from his eye continued to roll down his face, which became more serious as he spoke again, "Well, I should introduce myself." He waved his cup in the air, spilling tea. "The May Hire."

He froze. "Wait no, the May Hand. No..."

Then, he snapped his fingers. "March! That was it. The March Hare."

He looked back at Lam, her eyes wide.

"But you're madder than Hatter!"

He narrowed his eyes. "Yes... And?" But then he seemed to forget her and he looked around. "Is the good old Hatter around? I heard he would be!"

"Right here." Hatter, already in full view, walked over to his old friend and shook his hand. "It's good to see you, too."

"He's not all mad."

This time, Lam was glad to hear the voice beside her. The young joker had come around the table while Old Cheshire grabbed cups for everyone.

"When he fights or teaches, he's pretty sane," the joker's tone was low and soft, comforting in its truthfulness.

Lam looked down at her untouched food—the brown sugar in a lump in the middle. "Or he's just a different kind of mad. Like how you get when you fight."

 "You think I go mad?" Bright eyes flashed orange before beginning to dilate.

Lam paused to watch. The transition was fabulously fascinating, turning orange, to pink, to red, and finally to gold as the color was quickly taken over with pupil.

Her gaze dropped as her flush rose. "It's more like a part of you grows."

"Maybe you just see it then and he's always like that." Rudyard, making himself a cup of tea, put in with a less than neutral expression.

"I don't think so..." Again, Lam risked a glance to find the joker's eyes had returned to normal. "It's like you're someone else."

The joker stared at her for a very long time. Lam squirmed at the scrutiny until she realized that his eyes were unfocused.

Rudyard sat down between them. "Do you think that the March Hare is sane enough to teach you?"

"I think so. He is the greatest fighter." Lam wished she was as confident as her voice felt.

The young joker leaned over so she could see him, pretending to be hurt, but the effect wasn't the same with syrup dribbling down his face.

"Also, he knows how to use a battle axe." She relaxed at saying something she agreed with. "Do you know anyone else who uses one?"

Rudyard nodded, taking a sip of tea. Instantly, he began to cough and splutter. The joker smiled and took the cup, replacing it with Rudyard's actual cup of tea.

"How can you drink that? It's so sweet."

"Another one of my many talents." The joker downed the rest of what was in the cup.

"Or shortcomings," Mack said with a sage nod.

Lam nodded as well. "How will he survive in the real world?"

The joker opened his mouth to make a witty comeback, but just then the March Hare finished his tea and sat forward.

"Well now, I think it's time for me to see what you can do, little blooderfly."

～

"Do you already have an axe?"

Both jokers, Rudyard, and Lam were back on the ground

in a clearing not far from Mister Willow. Rudyard and the young joker sat off to one side, as close as the March Hare would let them.

Lam shook her head. "Sorry, what?"

"Your axe?" March Hare glared down at her with a strange mix of disappointment and disinterest.

"Oh, yes, I have it."

"Give it here."

Lam didn't want to, but she did as she was told. Hare took off the silk wrap and took in a sharp breath. "You again." His hand balled the fabric. Turning to Lam, he asked, "Why do you have this?"

"I found it." But that wasn't true. "Well, the joker found it for me." But it was hers. "In the castle of Hearts." For some reason she needed him to know it was rightfully hers. "Is there something wrong with it?"

"From a weaponry standpoint? Not at all." He ran his finger along the curved blade. "Its sharpness is unmatched by any other weapon in Hearts and can never grow dull. Also, it's made of Heart Gold." He let blood drip from his finger. "But... this blade has a long history. One that you might not want to hold."

Lam looked at the small smudge of blood that now ran along the blade. "It's mine now and I can't give it up."

"Loyalty...is seen as a good thing to blades." And with that, he gave the axe back. Then he swung an enormous axe off of his back. It was black from tip to hilt and more serrated than a bread knife. He caught her wide-eyed look.

"The weapons might be different in size and proportion, but the principles are the same. Are you ready to begin?"

Lam grabbed her axe with both hands and stood up straight. "Yes, sir."

"Good luck." The young joker waved jauntily.

"To start..." Hare reached forward and pulled her left hand off the upper half of the hilt. "Don't hold it like that."

Lam suddenly felt like she would need that luck.

"Lam, are you okay?" Mack asked with wide eyes.

Her hands were shaking so badly she couldn't get her spoon to her mouth. "Yes, but I do feel like I've been starved."

They had worked nonstop till dinner, a dinner Lam was now shakily crying over.

"You'll get used to it," the young joker said, guiding the spoon to her mouth.

"No, she will not," Rudyard said, glaring at him. "She will take breaks when she needs to."

The joker raised his hand in surrender. "I'm not saying it for my good," he said, pointing with his spoon dripping pie filling. "If she's going to make it through the next two games, she needs to know how to fight."

This silenced Rudyard, but he continued to glare at Cheshire. Hare left early, something about potions. And soon after, Old Cheshire went to put Shire to bed. The rest, afraid of having to clean up, left, leaving the joker alone again. Lam didn't even care it wasn't her room. She just cleaned her teeth and put on her nightgown. But this night, she wouldn't collect her dreams...

Dust lifted at her foot steps as Lam walked into a theater. Wooden beams creaked warnings and shattered stained glass hid behind tattered curtains, casting broken moon light on the stage. Blood spattered the dress that covered her and fire was tight in her throat as she stared at the young man on stage.

He was a performer—a muse, a poet—but that was not what he was known for. No, in fact, Lam didn't know him at all.

In his hands appeared a matchbox and stick, red match head on black sand, the fire somehow blinding even at the distance. Straightening, he lifted the match to eye level, though his face was covered with a mask. The white and gold heat rushed down to his ungloved fingers.

Matches and fire... the kitchens... the girl and the sick game a boy once played. Memories of Lam's past all seemed hidden in his act. Rushing forwards, Lam's velvet shoes pressed into plush, bloody carpet.

"Stop, you'll—"

Her words and the light were cut off as he flicked the match out. The fire took the moon with it, and left Lam in nothing but darkness.

"Are you scared of fire?"

Fingers brushed Lam's face and a scream tore at her heart. She could hear him at her shoulder, pulling another match out. Then it was at her face, pulling at her skin. Fire caught and her right eye was blinded. She stood still, frightfully still, as the fire tried to burn her lashes.

'Stay still enough, and they'll think you're already dead.'

Who had told her that? Who was holding a flame to her face?

"You are a good actor..."

Grabbing her arm, the boy spun her around. Suddenly, they were on the stage, and the moonlight was black, shining over a crowd of six.

Her mother sat with her hands folded in her lap—the picture of a queen, even as ropes tied her down. Her father held his chin high even as his legs shook. Mack looked like he had come back to reality only to find it was even worse than he had expected. Hatter, Rudyard, and the joker sat painfully still, the joker's eyes a solid black.

The masked boy leaned right next to her ear.

"Off with their heads." But it was in her voice and Lam felt her lips move, sentencing all the people she loved to death. It happened so fast, in one swing of an axe—her axe. Their lifeless bodies dropped to the ground. Screaming, she ran to them. Bile rose in her throat as she cried over the body of her brother. She tried to remember how she had become this, but there seemed to have been no life before she was cruel. The boy held out his hand and without meaning to, she took hold of it. His skin was cold but soft, like snow. Looking up at his mask, it felt as if the floor had dropped out beneath her and only her heart was falling. She knew that in this world he could have her sentence anyone to death and no one would question it. Here, she was Queen.

"This is one of the outcomes of the path you chose." Leaning in close, he whispered in her ear, "and do you know who made those paths?"

Lam's lips silently mouthed the word 'Storytellers.'

He started to laugh. Stepping away, he raised his arms as if he were a conductor. "Welcome, Queen, to your nightmare."

Suddenly, inches away, his mask practically touching her face, his finger ran over her hair pushing it back too hard. "Welcome to my game." His hands were covered in blood that began to drip down her head. "Have fun at yours."

EIGHT

Lam sat bolt upright, her eyes wide and void of light. Her chest started to rise and fall as she began to hyperventilate, tears running down her face. Suddenly someone was at her door, someone covered in blood. She saw him dying, the weight in her chest, the color of his eyes, and the blood on her dress. Or no, there was no blood on the joker as he ran over to her.

He grabbed her wrist, trying to calm her down, but this only made her cry harder. Then they both noticed the mask that she gripped in her hands. The same black and silver one the monster had worn, except now, where there had been no mouth, a large crack smiled up at her. It was only then that she fell silent.

The joker looked up at her, eyes wide and jaw slack. Lam felt like she had been shattered, no longer whole, but a part of her was in the process of hardening.

His eyes sharpened, the same way they did when he fought, turning the world into people and meaningless shapes, allowing him to focus. "No, no, no! Princess, talk to me!" He started to shake her, as unable to control himself as she had been a moment ago. "Please think about anything! Princess, tell— Tell me how old you are."

Lam looked up at him. At least now she was listening.

"I am sixteen."

"Good. Now…" His eyes returned to their normal state as he started to calm down. He scanned the room for inspiration. "What is your favorite food?"

"Meat-pie. But only when Hatter makes it." Her voice was soft and more steady.

"Good, good. And your favorite place?"

"The maze." A little life had come into Lam's eyes.

The joker tilted his head and started to pull her hands off of the mask. "What if I paint all of the flowers? Will it still be your favorite place?"

Lam smiled, letting him take her hands. "Yes, but you'd always be painting and you would never have tea with us."

"I'd find time." The joker's eyes ran over her face, trying to see her nightmares. She looked at the wall behind him and gasped. The sun had just come over the horizon, stretching his arms out over the sky as he woke. She rarely saw this side of the sun, the one that was still drowsy and not yet ready for the world. It was even rarer for her to see it shaded by leaves and peaking through trees.

Looking back at Lam, the joker smiled. "Do you want to go see it?"

She nodded and let him pull her to her feet. It was so strange how different he was to the boy from her dream. His hands were light on her arm, gliding her unsteady feet.

The sun grabbed her face and poured over her skin as they ascended on stairs to the top of the tree. It was even more beautiful from the tree line and Lam wasn't thinking about the drop. Slowly, she told him her nightmare as they watched the sun rise.

"Princess, do you know how hearts work?"

Lam was confused. It was such a strange thing to ask a girl who had just had a nightmare. "What do you mean?"

"Everyone has a type. That type determines how each person's heart can be broken." He ran a hand down his shirt as if he wanted to open his chest to show her what he meant. His hand made a fist and fell to his lap. "My heart is water. The closest I can get to having my heart broken is for it to freeze. The Hatters' hearts are made of glass. They can be broken and healed, each time with more metal between the shards, making it harder and harder to break." The joker looked at Lam to make sure she was still listening. "Your heart is made of clay. It can be shaped and changed without hurting you, but after the first firing, it's as fragile as glass. After the second, it's as hard as stone."

Lam's eyes held nothing but confusion.

"Some people are born with the ability to see hearts, and I'm one of them." Running a hand through his hair, he turned away. "Never mind. It's hard to explain." Quietly, he rose to stand, his invitation clear in the hand he barely lifted to her.

HER HANDS still shook while she walked. Lam wasn't exactly scared, her feelings fell somewhere between confusion and a dull sense of dread. She could see March Hare laughing through the doorway to the kitchen, his form slightly blocked by the joker walking in front of her.

Hare took one look at her eyes and pulled out an empty bottle. His movements were so swift; he brushed the nightmares into the flask before she could even open her mouth or flinch away. When the bottle was safely in his pocket, she was glad to have them off her face. It was a little easier to think.

Hare turned away and back to Old Cheshire, who held concern in the knit of his brow.

Wiping her nose, she sat down at the table, not sure what to do. Her feelings shifted to embarrassment and she dearly wished she could just go back to bed. A plate of bread-&-butterflies was pushed softly under her bowed head. Her eyes rose to see the joker holding another one for himself.

"Ever had these?" Smiling, he sat across from her.

Lam picked up one slice by its toasted corners. "I don't think so... Isn't it just toast?"

His smile widened. "That's almost true." He poured syrup onto her's before covering his in the stuff.

Tentatively, Lam lifted it to her mouth. The flavor was simple but unexpected, more rich than she would have guessed. "This is amazing! Where did you find more syrup?"

The joker looked up, surprised, an entire piece in his mouth. Swallowing it whole, he coughed to clear his throat. "This is from my personal collection." He smiled proudly and lifted up his bottle, the size of a normal cup. "From my birthday before last."

Lam felt a new level of appreciation for the food before her. Her vision blurred as she reflected on all of the kind things the joker had done for her.

"Hey, hey, hey..."

Her eyes glazed as her chin began to tremble.

"What's wrong? I promise it's safe to eat."

Lam looked up at him, tears running down her face. "I'm sorry, you've done so many things you didn't have to... And you took such good care of me... And you were trying to tell me something really important!" Her eyes dropped to her plate.

"Hey! It's ok!" He laid the backs of his hands on the table. "It's also kinda my job."

Lam's brows knit together as she looked up. The joker waved a hand up in the air. "I mean, we're usually not this direct, but my job as a joker is to make sure the royals are safe and the people are treated fairly." He smiled and gestured to Hare. "It's both our jobs."

Hare rose from the place he'd been leaning, talking with Old Cheshire. "It's also the only reason I'm here." He set his mug down on the table with a thud. "Though you better not take my time for granted, Little Queen."

"I'm not a queen." It was an instinctual response, one she had cultivated over the past decade of people referring to her as a young queen. She was not the queen; her mother was, her brother's future wife would be... But she was not.

"Really?" Hare's eyes shined with quiet amusement. "You could have fooled me."

LAM DRAGGED her feet almost as much as the joker when it was time to go. For him it was understandable. Though he'd spend most of his time doing chores, he would still be home with his family. Even as the others ate, the joker spent his time chasing his brother and pretending to be a dragon.

By the time Rudyard and Mack were in the carriage, he was only halfway ready and Lam was just getting in. Thankfully, Old Cheshire had already loaded the joker's very small number of things onto the carriage.

"Do you *want* me to leave?" the joker said, sounding a little hurt.

Old Cheshire sighed, "No, but I want you to win The Games, if one of your companions doesn't beat you to it." He gave Lam a wink.

The joker finally got into the carriage with a sigh. Once

they were out of sight of the clearing and the waving Cheshires, he turned from the window.

"You two need to fall asleep." His eyes passed over Mack to bounce between Lam and Rudyard.

"So the magic won't work?" Lam guessed.

The joker nodded. Rudyard huffed, but he did as he was told. It was incredible how quickly he could sleep, and sleep anywhere. She could remember a time she'd found him asleep in a pile of weapons while he was avoiding his tutor. She wished this memory would distract her, wished she'd focus on something fun and simple.

Instead, her eyes shifted between the magical, wonderful, slightly disturbing world outside and the boy across from her. Lam never caught his eyes, but every time she looked away, she felt them on her skin.

It brought a strange feeling, something she'd never really felt before—a mix of curiosity and a pull in her chest. Sure, she had found others attractive, she even fantasized about the lives she might have with them, but the way she felt towards the joker was something different...almost older.

As red began to stain her cheeks, she mentally chided herself and looked away for the eighth time. He was just a boy, but even the voice in her head couldn't believe such a blatant lie. Her wandering mind was brought back to reality with a sharp bump as the carriage went over the bridge to Diamonds. Wide-eyed realization stole her breath. Finally, her eyes met the joker's. His face was understanding and a little sad.

"Don't worry, most people who see Hare go a bit mad; it's nothing serious."

Lam pulled her mouth closed and into a smile, though she wasn't convinced. She felt the truth in every beat of her heart, in every breath she took, in how the world looked... that it had much more to do with her nightmare than Hare.

"I don't mind if I'm mad. Actually, I was planning on it." Confidence shifted her smile to a grin. "How else am I to become a joker?"

He nodded in an overly thoughtful way. "There's no way you could."

Taking in a slow breath, Lam decided to not tell her parents that she was mad. Or Rudyard. Maybe not even Hatter. Because, although Lam rarely lied, she was quick to hide the truth.

As they exited the carriage hours later, all she did was give her parents big hugs and tell them she'd had a lovely time.

"That's wonderful dear." Her mother patted her back. "And it's good to see you safe and home."

"Yes, is there anything you want to do before the game?" her father said with an infectious smile.

"I'd like to take a nap."

"A nap?" her mother asked, confused.

The king grabbed the hand of his wife. "Remember your first game?"

The queen smiled up at him, "I guess..." She looked down and saw how exhausted Lam looked. "Oh dear, you look beat. Go straight up to your room."

Still wearing her traveling clothes, she laid down on her soft, warm sheets that were not quite as comfortable as the joker's.

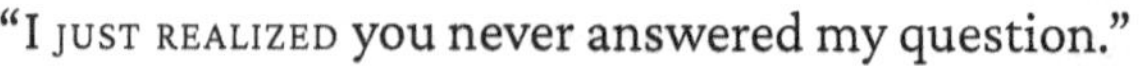

"I just realized you never answered my question."

Sheets, thick and far too many, began to suffocate Lam.

"Rather rude, you know..."

They were becoming scratchy, wounded and wounding like the voice that beat in her ears. "So I'll ask you something else."

She couldn't breath, couldn't see, could feel every fiber of the world around her. Then...space, a void, emptiness at her back. She was gripping on to the sheets she'd been pushing away moments ago.

"Tell me everything you fear."

And the sheets became scales as snakes became all that was holding her from an impossible fall.

"No, no, no."

One, a silver and black viper, dug into her arm, not just with its teeth, but its entire body. Her veins became venom as more brought their bodies to her flesh.

"No!"

It was pain like fire, burning her heart.

"Hearts, no." Her voice was weak, meek against the darkness.

Suddenly, a mask was in her face, one with crying eyes and a grin. "Hearts? Now those are certainly things to be feared." With half gloved hands and black throwing knives, the Storyteller stabbed into her chest.

L am sat up, shaking from the dream. "Joker?"

She was surprised that was the first thing to come to her. She didn't even know how she knew he was there. He faded into view, standing on her balcony in the late afternoon sun.

"Was it the same?" His voice was distorted by the glass doors between them.

She shook her head, feeling so alone. Picking up on her thoughts, he walked over to the door. He stood there, waiting, not even trying the handle. Lam moved to the door, resting her hand on the gold handle long enough for it to recognize her and open. They stood there a moment, as the door swung open and cold air blew in. Lam wondered if he was cold, if he ever got cold, if he liked the cold. In truth, she wondered a great deal about the joker. More than she should.

As he entered her room, his shoulder brushed hers, so softly she convinced herself she'd imagined it.

"Do you want to talk about it?" His eyes darted around the room to find something more helpful to say. "I personally don't like talking about them, but you—"

"I don't want to talk." Lam wished her voice wasn't so harsh. Her fingers cupped the edge of the bed curtain, pulling it back and letting the sheer fabric gather at one end. Sighing, she sat back down on her bed. "I don't want to talk about it."

The joker was silent as he moved to sit next to her. It was uncanny how he could move with no sound. In his lap, he twisted and untwisted a vine that Lam had seen climbing up the walls of his old room.

"You know, when I was little, Cheshire never knew what to do when I had a nightmare." Shaking his head, the joker looked to the ceiling. "He would ask me, 'What's wrong, what's wrong?' over and over as I cried." Her eyes rose to his face and the smile that twitched at his lips. "My favorite thing he did was tell me stories." Blue and yellow eyes shifted to red and orange as he looked to her. "Would you like me to tell you a story?"

Smiling, Lam leaned on the post of her bed. "I would love that."

"There once was a brave—" he moved to sit, propped on the opposite post, "but not the bravest—Joker."

Lam felt her shoulders relax at his voice and her fingers began to twist the curtains, the same way his did around the vine.

"He traveled all around Cards and one day he came to a wall of glass. When he looked through, he saw what you'd expect: a reflection of the Forest. But that wasn't quite true, because he didn't show up against the trees. Curious, the Joker rested his hand on the glass. Before he knew it, he found himself on the other side. Behind him was his bag and the Forest he'd just come from. For it was no reflection, but a pathway. He went all along the mirror trying to find the end, but it was so long he would have to walk for days and days before he reached the end. After only one day without any difference, he gave up and journeyed farther into the strange land. Once he had walked for a little while, he came to a hedge wall so thin you could stick your finger through to the other side. At first, he thought it was a maze, but it only ever lead to equally sized squares. Each square had eight doors, one in each wall and one in each corner. This was the first time anyone had crossed the Looking Glass."

His eyes followed the twists of the vine as if it was feeding off of the story he'd been taught in his childhood. Lam briefly wondered why he'd chosen this story. She'd heard it a million times. But this time she got lost in it. This time there where colors in the words.

"After many adventures, the Joker returned to the Deck of Cards. He told the High King and Queen of Cards of his findings and of the Kings and Queens of Chess. At first, peace was formed between the Deck and Board. The problem was that the mirror swayed and the border kept moving. War broke out, the mirror was broken, and The Games were created."

It was odd, being told one of the most important historical events in Wonderland in such a simple way. Her face quirked into a teasing grin. "I think you're missing some things."

He waved his hand. "Details. I got all the important stuff: the Joker, the war, The Games." He looked down at a non-existent watch in his hands. "And I do believe that we have one of those games to go to now." Pretending to snap his watch closed, his eyes rose to hers. "Hatter is the reason I'm here. He needed me to get you and tell you to stop sleeping like a door-mouse. Are you ready?"

Lam nodded, the color back in her face. "Are you going to get dressed, too?"

"Do you dare to suggest that this piece of art is not what I will go to The Games of Kings and Queens in?" The joker puffed out his chest, spreading his arms to show the worn clothes from Old Cheshire.

Snorting, Lam tried to look serious. "All will tremble in fear before the mighty pauper."

He gave her a fake sour look and stood. "Come on, Your Highness, I do believe that Lord Hatterman is ready with your apparel." His hand elegantly fell towards her.

Resting her hand in his, she let him pull her from the bed. "*Now* you address me like you should?" She raised her eyebrows.

He bowed his head and kissed her hand. "Should I always?"

The sensation of blooderflies in her stomach flitted though her. Blushing, she looked away and to a small, broken bleeding heart resting on her pillow. Again, the floor of her chest seemed to fall out and take her heart with it. But just as swiftly as the feeling came, the joker picked the flower up and set it in his pocket.

"Each Storyteller can only tell one path; you can choose which to follow."

"Joker..." Her voice was hesitant, and her hands twitched at her sides. "Do you ever have nightmares...about...him?"

He looked at her eyes, an icy pain in his, like he had been hit too many times to be hurt. "Every night... I just stopped screaming." He said it so softly that she could barely hear him.

"What does he tell you?" Lam whispered, giving him the option to pretend that he hadn't heard.

"'Love is like heat, it will burn you down as easily as it will keep you from dying.' 'Only a fool gives away his heart, for with it he gives away his mind.' 'Every love story either ends in heartbreak or death.'" He looked over at Lam and shrugged. Only then did she really notice how tired he was.

"Sometimes we just sit there countering each other's words."

"What are some of the arguments that you make?"

Turing to the door, the joker spoke gently. "I would rather die in the shadow of someone greater than try and take their life for my own. A servant without a heart has more than a king with his own." The joker shrugged, moving uncomfortably. "I'm not really a poet. We should probably go see Hatter."

CHAPTER

TEN

When they arrived, Rudyard was already dressed in a red vest over a ruffled white shirt with simple pants. Hatter was working at his sewing machine, the pins jumping out as he came to them.

"Tea is on the table. I'm almost done with your dress, Lam. Cheshire, your outfit is already in the dressing room." Hatter never looked away from his work. Even if the whole world was on fire, Lam doubted he would leave a project unfinished.

Lam sat down while the joker went to go get dressed, though she only needed to wait a moment.

"There. Done!" Hatter said, flourishing the dress off the sewing table. The only thing she could see was that it was red and flowy. Lam took the dress in her arms and walked to the second dressing room.

Once in the room, she took off her clothes and slipped on the dress. Everything about it was wonderful and versatile. It had a fitted bodice form without being constricting and sleeves that could either be on or off the shoulder. Gold detailing shown on the mock spine, running down the long full skirt, and in the ribcage around her torso. It came with a gold locket that had a faint beating when she laid it on her skin as well as a pair of heart shaped earrings.

She and the joker emerged from the dressing rooms at the same time. He, too, was in red and gold. He wore a full suit: shirt, waist coat, pants, tie, and jacket all in deep red. The flaps of the jacket were piped in gold and his cuffs were gold as well. Unlike Rudyard, the joker looked natural in suits. The most striking thing of it all was the gold mask covering the lower half of his face, shaped like a skull.

Both of them finished their inspection of each other at the same time and turned to Hatter, who nodded.

"You two will look lovely as teammates." He paused, as if considering a new song on the turntable. "Unless...you don't wish to be teammates, then it will be quite...ah...embarrassing."

The joker tipped back to Lam, a teasing grin hidden behind the gold. "I would hate to embarrass a princess."

Lam made a face, though a smile soon took over. "I would hate to wrong a joker."

Giving the joker a sour look, Rudyard led the way down the stairs before Hatter stopped the other two.

"I almost forgot, Hare told me to give you these." Hatter held out his hand. Resting in his palm sat two glass vials the color of liquid gold, the color of Hare's eye.

"What are they?" Lam asked as she picked one up.

"He said that they might help with your sleeping problem." Hatter's gaze swept up to the joker.

Lam hadn't noticed the gold finger-bones that guarded the backs of the joker's hands till he reached forwards and snatched the bottle. "Now he makes this?! ...No offense Lam."

"None taken." Lam, too, looked up at Hatter. "Why now?"

"He needed a nightmare given without a word."

The joker shook his head and started to laugh, though it was obvious he was feeling a lot more than just humor. "Thank you both. And Hatter," he looked down at the bottle, "tell Hare that if this works, I owe him the world."

ONCE AGAIN, two royals, one junior adviser, and one joker piled inside Hatter's carriage. As they trundled along, Lam thought of the fire under their feet, pushing water into steam and making them move. She did not think of the joker sitting across from her, or the edge of her dress pressed to his knee. Lam didn't even bother to consider the soft humming in his throat as he stared out of the window, because she wasn't concerned with him.

Lam just sat with her hands in her lap and her eyes on the tiny space of floor that was visible, while Mack and Rudyard chatted. A bump shifted all of them an inch and suddenly her space of floor was gone and sunlight bounced off the gold mask sitting next to the joker.

Moving to look out of the window, she found him studying her. He didn't just look at things, he assessed them, counted them. His eyes flicked over her face as he counted her freckles. An arduous and useless task, but still he did it. With lips silently parting, tongue forming numbers Lam had never bothered to know. His eyes dipped to her neck and it was as if heat tracked his movements.

"You won't be able to count them all."

His lips stilled around thirty-four. "And why is that?"

"I—" The heat was no longer contained by his gaze. Somehow he seemed completely unaffected. His eyes were still a mixture of greens, blues, and browns.

"I have freckles all over my body."

Finally his eyes shifted, turning a bright pink as they moved to the window.

Rudyard's eyes also moved, though his narrowed. "I hope for your sake you weren't staring at my sister inappropriately."

"I would never." Though the words seemed ironic, they were said with honesty.

For the rest of the ride, he stared out the window and Lam watched the floor. When they arrived at the field—the same one as before—Lam couldn't help feeling a creeping, sick feeling. It was in her limbs as she stepped from the carriage and in the air she sighed out. Her gaze moved from the tunnel they were about to enter to the stands now set high above.

"Are you coming?" Rudyard made a point of raising his eyebrows as Mack and Hatter walked towards the stands.

"Something feels off." When she looked back at Rudyard she saw blood on his leg and pain on his face. Her eyes shuttered closed and when she looked again he was back to normal except a shining bit of sunlight that looked like gold on his arm. Her vague feeling became a shiver as she followed Rudyard and the joker into the tunnel.

"Hello, Lam."

Nerves already high, Lam shrank back and twisted towards Teon, reaching for a weapon she didn't have. His whole body stiffened, the planes of his face becoming rigged and hard.

"Oh!" Lam made up for his stiffness by letting hers go. "Hello, Teon."

A soft smile grazed his face, but his shoulders were still held in tension. "Is everything alright?"

She didn't know why she felt it, but something wasn't right about this place. "Yes, I'm just a little nervous."

Something warm and strong met the back of her arm, but

Lam didn't flinch. A different feeling was calming her racing heart.

"Hello, Knight." The joker titled his head till it was almost touching Lam's. "Is there something you wanted with my partner?"

"I—" Teon's expression went from annoyed to shocked. "What do you mean?"

"I mean—"

"That this is going to be a team game!" Lam cut in, taking a firm step away from the joker, creating the distance that propriety demanded. "Or, that's what we were told. The—" Once again, Lam stumbled around his title. "He has been my weapons teacher for the past couple of days and thought it would be a good idea if we worked together."

With a flourish, the joker lifted his mask to his lips. "I thought it was a group decision."

"Well..."

He was disarming in a way that made her more curious than scared.

"Yes..." The admission felt like a failure and a success at the same time, in a game Lam only half wanted to play. "I suppose so."

Once again, the call of the Tweetles' horns saved her. They rang out over the tunnel as the two stepped inside.

"Good afternoon—"

"Contestants."

"We hope—"

"You're all—"

"Well rested."

The twins smiled, but it did nothing for the fear starting to creep back over Lam's shoulders and she turned away from both Teon and the joker.

"Today is the—"

"Second game!"

Day's tone became comically dark. "A game that most of you—"

Deevon's voice was childishly sad. "Will not win."

There was a pause where the girls closed their eyes.

"But..." One of Day's eyes opened and she swiveled it to look at Deevon.

"All of you..." Deevon, too, opened one eye and peered at her twin.

The two chanted in unison, "Will have an equal chance."

"First,"

"Find a partner—"

"From an allied kingdom." They clasped their two hands together.

Lam felt the warm weight of the joker's hand in hers. Her heart was beating, bleeding into the rest of her, but even as she squeezed his hand, she kept her eyes forward and her mind clear.

"Now—"

"Don't loose them."

"If only one of you—"

"Gets out—"

"Nether of you—"

"Will pass."

The wording was odd and ominous but Lam stayed focused as they explained the rules.

"Once you are in the maze—"

"Any injury you acquire—"

"Will be your own."

"If you are—"

"In real danger—"

"You will be pulled from the game—"

"And automatically lose."

The two smiled as they turned and walked into the vine covered tunnel.

"You have—"

"Until sunset."

"Good—"

"Luck."

The words echoed over one another, bouncing till they vanished.

Tick.

Tick.

Tick.

"Princess," the joker drew out the word as he drew closer and started to push Lam forwards, "I think you go first."

Lam didn't want to go first, didn't want all the eyes angrily staring at her or the tunnel seeming to open its mouth for her. Lam didn't like the darkness or the weight on her shoulders… But she didn't like much about the situation, and she was only holding up the line.

With feigned confidence, she marched forwards, the joker's hand in hers, and his smile lifting the hairs on her neck.

"I can feel your grin," she whispered between gritted teeth as they ducked through the vines.

He chuckled.

Heat chased away the darkness as torches lit themselves on the walls. Before them, seventeen different openings stood. Not missing a beat, the joker pointed to the far right tunnel. "We should go down that one."

Lam made a face, brightened by the red in her cheeks. "Why?"

Shrugging, he started to walk towards it. "I like it."

"And what if I don't." Lam's free hand fisted.

"Then you can go another way." The gold skull seemed to

grin at Lam as he let go of her hand, turned, and walked backwards into the tunnel. "Who knows, we might meet up before time runs out."

A cracking sound broke beneath his feet and he threw out his arms to hold himself suspended in the air as the floor of the tunnel crashed in a hole.

"To be fair—"

Marching forwards, Lam grabbed his arm as the second group entered the room. "My turn."

Pulling him from his precarious position, Lam saw a golden light on the floor of the tunnel just to the left. It was faint and as soon as her feet met it, the light turned to smoke. Still, the path seemed far better, and they were loosing their lead.

Lam moved gently. She was always graceful, but now she was tentative. Each of the three games got harder and harder, with a higher chance of getting injured. The final game was always hand-to-hand combat between the remaining contestants, but the other two games were different every year.

Firelight flickered off of Lam's thoughts as they moved farther from the sounds of other people.

It was only when the crackling of torches became distinct that Lam realized she couldn't hear the joker at all. Frantic, she gripped his hand tighter and twisted to stare at him. "What's wrong?"

He wasn't hovering and she could clearly see his feet fall to the floor again and again as they speed walked. "What?"

"With you?"

"Well now..." He twisted his face into something sour. "I'm not sure I know, myself."

Lam rolled her eyes even as a smile tipped her lips. "Not overall... Why can't I hear you?"

"Ah... That would be from years of having to sneak

around." He took a step from her as they entered a sunlit room, filled with books.

Letting go of his hand, Lam wandered to the shelves as she asked, "Why did you have to sneak? Old Cheshire didn't seem anything to be scared of."

The joker's laugh bounced of the books he went to inspect. "He is, but that's not why."

Lam's fingers traced the spines of Forest tales and folklore as her eyes flitted to the joker's back.

"I have an older brother. To be fair, I have a lot of older brothers..." His hand stilled on an encyclopedia of talking animals and sentient creatures of the world. "He... Story-tellers, I don't even know if he's still alive..." The hand fisted and he turned to Lam. "I..." But the look on her face made him pause.

Her eyebrows went up as her lips parted. "And..."

"And..." He couldn't stop the blackness overtaking the red and even the purple in his eyes. "We should stay focused." He stepped over to her and got a finger in his face for it.

"For now." Lam felt deceived—lied to, almost. The joker got to get away with knowing so much more about her than she knew about him. Her finger fell as she turned back to the shelf. "Tomorrow you have to tell me more."

"You want to know more?" He said it like a trap, like a wolf in sheep's clothing, but as she noticed pink and purple twisting in his eyes, she saw only a sheep pretending to be a predator.

"Yes. Is that a problem, Joker?"

His nose wrinkled like it always did when he was truly pleased. "Not at all, Princess." His hand reached past her and pulled a book entitled *The Complete Guide to Games, Wars, and Gardening.*

The book practically fell open as soon as it was in his

hand, and out of it dropped six pages. Crouching, Lam lifted them while the Joker flipped through the book.

"Sadly, the rest is just about war and gardening." His eyes fell to her and the pages in her hands. "What are those?"

"Maps." A wry smile was filled with a sigh, "All slightly different maps."

Each one was distinctly similar, with the same entrance and seventeen tunnels, but what was along each of the tunnels was completely different. Some had pits of fire on one map and a pristine garden with carnivorous plants in the next. Even their own chosen path changed in each one, though all had this room.

"I don't get it, why give us a map if we don't know if it's real."

"We can never know if it's real." The joker lifted one of them and studied it. A smile shown in his eyes as he looked past the page to her. "I bet they're all telling the truth."

Lam stood and stared at the maps in their hands. "How can they all be telling the truth?"

Gently, he swept the five maps in her hands on top of the one he held. "They don't need to tell the whole truth, just enough to be valuable."

Lam leaned over his shoulder and he lined up each path. "So something has to tell the truth to be valuable?"

"At least a little bit." His hands rose and brought her gaze with it, showing shining dots where every page had a puncture in the exact same spot.

"How did you..." Her question died between her lips as the joker twisted back towards her. His hands fell as his eyes filled with a strange mix of colors. The pink she'd expected, the red, too, but the green and purple were strange to see. His breath brushed her cheek through his mask and she was reminded of the stands, sitting high above and staring down at them. She saw her parents, her mother with field glasses pressed to the bridge of her nose as she searched for Lam. She saw her father, stiff in his chair with one of his half frowns. She saw the Prince of White Chess…

Lam shoved his shoulder and stepped back, guarding herself with distance. But it wasn't the White Prince, and she didn't hate or fear this boy who now had purple dripping over his view. "I—" But he was already looking away, and Lam felt blooderflies beating their wings at her back.

Lam's first instinct was to curl in, to berate herself in the comfort of her own mind, but she had done that before. This time, Lam grabbed the joker's arm and waited till he looked her in the eyes. "I'm sorry, I was just reminded of someone I don't like and…" The words still stuck in her head and on her tongue. There were too many places for them to get hung up.

"Is he smart?"

The question surprised Lam so much that all she could do was blink. "Only in the worst way."

"So you like me more?"

Snorting, Lam let go of his arm. "Of course. I hate him."

With yellow eyes, the joker led to way to where the first dot had glowed in the corner of the room. "But hate isn't the opposite of love." His fingers began to trace the book shelves.

"No, but surely thinking about someone in any way other than hate is better?"

His hand caught on a latch and a smile spread over his face.

"Sure, but think of all the time you spent not thinking about me." Then he pressed into the wall and…nothing happened.

Shoo-ing him out of they way, Lam looked at the small latch he'd uncovered. It was made of the same soapstone as the rest of the book shelves, but was engraved with three rings. "Well," Lam continued to talk as her hands felt the phase of the moon tripled beneath her fingers, "I will have you know, I thought about you a lot before I knew you." The new moon clicked into place above its doubles.

"You did?"

Lam pressed into the wall of books and turned. "Of course, I've always wondered who our joker was." Then she stepped into a room full of birds.

CHAPTER

ELEVEN

No ground met Lam's feet. "Hear—" Her curse was cut short as she began to pitch forwards. A hand latched on to hers and she was pulled to the joker. "-ts..." It was a sigh, a puff of air, so calm in contrast to the beats in her chest.

His free hand caught her shoulder and pulled her till they were both standing on the small step before the massive drop.

"Do you think it's fatal?"

"No." She felt unstable with one free hand swinging by the void, but she was already holding him too much. "That would be far too dangerous."

The joker's fingers pressed into her dress's fabric and golden bones as he turned his gaze to the birds. "Hallow— Mmmmm" His expletive became a groan behind gold, "Of course it's cross crows."

"What are cross crows?"

The birds flying back and forth in the red room looked normal to Lam, and already she'd become distracted with the human-sized cages suspended in a line.

"They're nasty little creatures. It's said that a murder of crows once annoyed a Blood Weaver so much that she cursed them to only be able to move either north and south or east and west."

Lam forced herself to look back at the joker. "What makes them so bad?"

"They've never forgiven humanoids and will hunt anyone that moves in their line of flight."

Lam turned from him again and scanned the three cages. "How high can they fly?"

The joker followed her gaze. "Not to those cages."

The cages were evenly spaced, leading to an equally small platform overlooking the darkness below.

"Do you think this path knows who is on it and makes it hard for them in particular?"

The joker slipped his arms from her and moved towards the near cage, pulling his arms from the sleeves of his blazer. "Not likely. They put me in this room, didn't they?" He turned to the wall, his eyes scanning its smooth, red surface. "Would you mind if I carried you on my back?"

"What?" Her question was asked before Lam had even really registered his. "You want to carry me? Up the wall?" Lam clarified.

Shaking out his arms, the joker tilted his head to one side. "It will be difficult, but I can walk on any surface that can hold my weight. Once we reach the top, we can just walk over to the other side of the room." Grinning, he turned to her, eyes shinning with yellows and blues. "Or, possibly, we can just run along the wall."

The idea was exciting, but also worrying to Lam's more rule abiding side. "Isn't that cheating?"

The joker pressed one foot to the wall as if to test it. "This whole game is learning how to cheat, like with the map. Its not about playing fair."

"Fine." His plan was inescapably more appealing than swinging from cage to cage over a murder of crows. Still, the wall stared down at them with sinister grace. "Are you sure you can carry me up."

"Of course." His fingers flexed, ready to hold her. Suddenly the intimate nature of what he was about to do seemed to strike him. "But I could carry you in front if you'd prefer that."

Silently she nodded, flushing enough to make her neck feel hot. Gently, he swept one of his arms behind her skirt and up, hooking her knees on his elbow, his other hand caught her far shoulder as she started to tip towards the void.

The joker lifted one leg and Lam's world turned. Her scream was sharp and quickly buried in jacket. As everything went sideways, Lam focused on the scent now strong in her nose. In general, the joker carried little smell, but this close, Lam was filled with sweat and something both fresh and forest-y. Lam could picture the plant—a bush of green leaves that she would pick and eat as a child.

When had she done that...?

The world tipped again before Lam could place the smell. Her feet were set on the ground and Lam stepped away with a gasp. Suddenly, everything was too bright, blinding her and making her forget the smell.

"It's alright." Hands grabbed hers and things started to focus.

They stood on a wall that was three feet wide and stretched into other walls of similar width. From there, the maze seemed rather straight forward—boxed off rooms leading out, all filled with various challenges. The truly worrying part of it all was...

"It's huge!" Lam gasped, lacing her fingers with the joker's as she twisted to look at the beginning, only a few dozen yards back, then turned to the hundreds of yards yet to come.

"Which means we really need to hurry." The joker's eyes were sharp as he stared at the falling sun. "Most of the games with no clear cut off point end at sundown, so that gives us no more than three hours."

TWELVE

The sun seemed to be growing larger the longer Lam stared at it. Seconds were ticking, clicking faster and faster, but that didn't make sense. Her eyes dipped to her feet, and the stone, now shaking, as panels of the wall were pulled away.

Her arms were yanked and the joker slipped his fingers from hers to catch her waist. The ground was dropping out below. He lifted her from the changing stone. The clicking grew faster as the top of the stone wall flipped, one panel at a time till it was completely covered in spikes two inches tall.

Turning from the disturbing ground, Lam's nose met the joker's mask. "We really need to stop doing this." Her tone was shockingly light, quickly contrasted by the joker's.

"Almost dying or holding onto each other?" The half joke was strained by her weight and the inches he was lifting them.

"Both. Now, I think if you lower us slowly, the spikes are close enough to each other for us to stand on."

He made a noncommittal hum, but began to descend. Sharp pressure was driven in to the base of their shoes but, as

Lam had guessed, the spikes held their weight. Letting go of her breath, Lam relaxed her arms and tilted her body from the joker. His arms fell from her as he lifted one shoe and turned to look out along the wall. Its entire length was covered in the same stone spines, but the adjacent wall was simple wood.

Haltingly, Lam lifted her right foot. The leather sole of her left shoe bent around the spikes before she could get her other down again. Before her, the joker calmly stepped over the spines, barely touching them.

"Why don't you just float?"

His head twitched at her words, but he didn't turn back as he spoke, "Because it's hard."

One step, then the next, her soles in pain. "Why?"

"Just because I *can* float doesn't mean it takes no effort. I'm still using my body, so it's a lot more like doing a plank than laying down."

"Are all your powers like that? Like walking on the wall earlier?"

His shoulders lifted to cradle his modesty. "Kind of. Walking on a wall is more like walking up a steep incline rather than climbing the wall." The joker's shoulders fell in sync with his next step. "But everything's easier in the Forest, so if I were to walk up a wall there, it would feel like normal walking, and floating feels just like standing."

Lam studied the sharp lines cut by his shirt. According to Old Cheshire, the joker hadn't been home in months and he'd been living on his own for two years. How much of that time had he lived in the Forest? Had he been there at all after leaving his family?

'More importantly, how long have you known him and how long are you going to make him suffer?'

She'd known him for such a small amount of time, but

even without knowing much about him, Lam wanted to help the joker.

"Cheshire." The name felt strange in her mouth, even as a mutter. Would it sound more right if she said it clearly? Her face flushed and she looked up from the studded path to find the joker's muscles were tensed again.

"I thought you weren't going to make a habit of saying it."

"And I won't."

'How long are you going to make him suffer?'

She didn't want him to suffer at all. "I was just thinking about the thing you need from me."

"I don't need anything." His words were too clipped to be honest.

Lam didn't bother watching the ground as she turned on to the wood wall. "But Old Cheshire-"

Coming to a halt, the joker pivoted back to her. "Shouldn't have said anything."

"But if I'm hurting you..."

Black and an awful amount of purple filled the space left by the joker's slitting eyes. "You can't. It's not something you can just give to me."

Lam half expected the purple to start dripping onto his cheeks. "But..." her voice seemed small next to the pain he was burying, "you do need it."

The joker reached forwards and grabbed her hand. "Would you give me this?"

Her slender fingers curled in shock. "What?"

"How about your eyes?" He stepped closer til his shoes were touching hers. "Or you teeth?" A warning ran up her spine. "Would you give me your bones if I asked?"

"N-no, why would you..."

He dropped her hand and brought space between them. "Then don't ask. What I need is none of your concern."

She could almost feel him falling away as his guard rose. She'd never seen this side of him.

I've only known him for a week. I haven't seen most of him.

Red shame clouded in her cheeks as they started to walk across the wall. She looked down to the rooms on either side. The room to their right, the path they had come from, was filled with boulders and jagged stones while the room to the left was home to a ginormous tea set. Lam's feet carefully tread the space between, half absent from the game. Dark wood creaked beneath her, though it had stood silent for the joker.

Was she heavier than him? She doubted it, his muscle was lean but as she had held him, she'd felt a weighty strength in his movements. He had to be floating, but if it worked like he said, he had to be getting tired.

The wood groaned again and Lam switched from walking to move more softly, as one of her instructors had taught. Still, the wood moaned below her.

"Joker, I-"

A splintered piece of wood shot up as the rest of the long board began to bend. With a frantic gaze, Lam took in the three boards that made up the top of the wall.

The joker, who had made it to the next board, whirled to her. "Lam!"

Fractured wood shot up around her feet even as a grin spread over her face. "You said my name."

Cursing, he moved forwards, but Lam threw out her hands.

"Don't come onto the board." Her heart was in her ears and blood was pressing behind her eyes, but still, she took in one slow breath. With her eyes shut, the cracking wood sounded like cracking ice.

'Remember, Lam,' her mother's hands had been warm on her

cheeks, even if her gold fingers were as frozen as the snow around,
'You must never go out onto the ice without your brother. Even if
you fall in, he can see and guide you out.'

Lam's eyes shot open as another piece of wood split. "You're staying here."

"What?!"

Her breath fell from her lips, not cold anymore. "I'm going to fall and there's nothing you can do to stop it. But if you stay up here, you can help guide me through the rest of the challenges."

"How?!" Black anger mixed with orange in his eyes.

Her smile was starting to hurt but she pulled it even wider. "I can't figure out everything."

A final bit of wood was driven into Lam's foot before the board collapsed in on itself. Even though Lam was terrified of heights, she rather loved the feeling of falling. Blood rose to her tongue as she counted,

One

T—

Hard porcelain stood ready to cradle the player unfortunate enough to fall. Lam tumbled down the teapot's spout, feet over elbows, into the warm liquid below.

CHAPTER

THIRTEEN

Out of all the things Lam thought she might do in her life, drowning in a pot of tea was not one of them. The warm, caramel liquid filled her nose and ears, making her splutter and gasp. As a small child, Lam had been relentlessly coached on swimming, till she could dive to the bottom of their loch and swim to the other shore without help. Somehow, all that knowledge seemed to be spilling out of her as the tea soaked into her dress.

"Princess!" The call was tinny and small, reflected in the porcelain.

Lam's muscle memory kicked in and she began to tread water. "Joker!" Her voice seemed loud in its echo, but no reply came. "JOKER!"

"Are you good?"

The question was so strange, she snorted. "What kind of question is that?" Slowly, she moved to swim under the open space at the top of the teapot.

The joker's tiny hands cupped his tiny mouth as he shouted. "The kind that needs an answer!"

"I'm well. Thank you for asking. And you?"

His arms fell at his side and she could almost feel the color of his eyes. "Good enough." Already, his voice was starting to scratch and for once Lam was glad for her speech tutors.

"You can't keep shouting like that."

"I know!" Frustration brought his hand to his hair as Lam scanned the inside of the pot.

It was a squat thing, around ten yards in diameter and probably seven tall, the tea sitting at three yards. Swimming to one wall, Lam inspected the white structure.

Her knuckles tapped against the ceramic. It had a thick, heavy sound, far too strong to break with her fist.

"I'm going to have to swim down and see if there's anything at the bottom."

The joker called something after her, but she ignored it as she flipped and dove down. Her body cut through the water even as her dress tried its best to slow her down. With her eyes closed, Lam had to rely on feel, tracing the smooth porcelain with her hands.

Her chest began to constrict. Her body shouted at her to take a breath. But Lam felt close, so close to solving this current puzzle. Her hand smacked into something large and sharp. Her blood was spilling into the tea as a thrill ran through her. Grabbing the thing with both hands, Lam swam to the surface. Her mouth was barely out of the water before the thing pulled her back down with its weight. Her eyes only just opened, but she caught sight of what she was holding.

Lam sank to the bottom with a full breath of air, a giant, sharpened spoon, and half a plan. The seconds had felt precious before and now they were vital—choking her as she lifted the spoon and stabbed into the wall of the pot. Again and again, she hit the ceramic, trying desperately to crack the wall. But her movements were slow in the liquid and air was running thin.

'You are weak.' Purple eyes, light and ringed in pale lashes, glared over his food. His smile was loud in her head, pushing tears to glaze her cheeks, 'But it's for the best, I always wanted someone...'

The spoon slammed through the porcelain, and Lam was pushed out. Ceramic and silver cut Lam's arms as she was spat out onto the tablecloth.

Lam, too, spat—spat out the tea in her mouth and the bitter memory of the White Prince.

"Princess."

The unnecessarily formal title sent Lam shaking with relief. "I'm..." Her lips trembled with a smile as she flipped to lay on her back. "I'm good."

She couldn't see him through the tea still clinging to her lashes and the bright afternoon sun, but she heard him shout down to her, "Then get moving."

Her eyelids and shoulders shot up. "Excuse me?"

Sun sparked off his mask, now in his hands, and pointed her eyes to his grin. "You heard me. Games don't wait for any queen."

It was a common phrase in Cards, but still Lam couldn't help grumbling, "I'm not a queen," as she stood on bloody legs. Only then did they both really take in her state—the long gashes on her arms and the red cuts waving between her leg hairs. "Well, aren't I a bloody mess?" Her lips quirked and she began to walk in the direction she hoped would bring her to the end of this game.

"How bad is it?" The joker was walking too, keeping in stride with her from above.

"Fine."

"Nobody says that when things are fine."

Lam shook the tea from her sopping curls and pulled one from her face. "And you're not supposed to talk back to a Princess."

"I could say the same to you."

Lam stepped onto a saucer, still smiling so much it hurt. "You're a princess?"

"You know what I mean."

"I don't think I do." It lasted a moment, her eyes moved from the lip of the saucer as she stepped off and found him, but, as she did, the world was suddenly tipped.

"Cheshire: seven, Lam: four. Good use of surprise and cutting off breathing."

The joker rolled his eyes from under her as she stood with one foot planted on his mouth. He said something that was muffled by her shoe.

"What was that?"

Her feet stumbled as they met the table cloth. What, indeed? Often her memories were so clear she felt like she was there, but that had never happened...

"Are you—"

"If you ask me if I'm good one more time, I will stop talking." Blinking hard, Lam watched the pattern of the cloth, the wetness of her shoes, anything to ground her to the moment. Once she'd regained her thoughts, she looked back up at the joker. "Can you walk ahead to check what's in the next room?"

He gave a small nod before running forwards and returning with stiff shoulders. "How do you feel about dragons?"

"That they don't exist."

She couldn't tell much about him from the distance, but she felt him about to argue before switching terms, "How do you feel about jabberwocks?"

Lam's brows fell as she trudged to the wall covered in bright paper. A door sat, crowned with green moulding and a shining gold handle. There was no correct answer to how she felt about jabberwocks, but she did feel like there was no point in waiting.

A roar greeted her, and someone shouted, "Whoever you are, get down!"

Lam crouched and looked up into eyes of flame. It was a beast with black scales and saliva dripping from its spiked jaw. Her training sent her diving into a roll as the jabberwock smacked its head into the door, shattering it into splinters.

Jumping to her feet, Lam stared around at the small group of people standing there. A girl with dark skin and her halo of hair now matted with blood, a second girl with long braids dyed red at the ends, a boy in a jewel studded suit and...

"Here—" A sword flew at her, "Can you— Lam!?" The final fighter turned and stared at her with red eyes, leg bloody, and pain hidden behind his commanding attitude.

Lam snatched the sword out of the air. "Rudyard?"

Things started clicking into place as she recognized Wesley and the two Princesses of Red Chess. But just then, the jabberwock started to shake out its head and turn back.

Jabberwocks were not dragons—they had no fire, no venom, no acid, and no wings—but they did have a bite worse than a shark and a tail lined in thorns. They had few weaknesses, too. Jabberwocks were not as impenetrable as the stories claimed. Any weapon, whether gold or steel, could pierce its hide with enough force and if its throat or mouth was blocked in any way, it would lose the drive to hunt.

Lam raised her sword and stared it dead in its flaming eyes. This one was nothing more than a baby, probably a year or year and a half at most. Lam didn't dare look way, for a jabberwock will only hunt whomever is staring into their eyes...and everyone else seemed to have already taken their turn. Even so, she let herself take in the thick chains around its ankles and the glass roof high above.

"Where in Underland is Cheshire!?" Rudyard shouted.

Lam gritted her teeth into a grin. "Up."

And as she said it, a sound like thunder and a rain of glass drew everyone's eyes but Lam's and the jabberwock's. Lam had seen aerialists perform for kings and queens, but the way the joker moved was better than any of them. He flipped once, twice, then landed in the space right behind the jabber-wock's head, driving his weapon into its cheek. Swinging down, the joker held on to nothing more than his half embedded blade. He pushed off thin air and stabbed the blade deeper and through the other side of its mouth.

The fire that was its eyes began to burn low as it collapsed to its stomach.

The joker dropped from the spear, then shook off the red spit and black blood before turning to Rudyard. "Here."

Lam raced forwards and punched him in the arm. "Are you mad! I wanted you on the wall! What are we going to do now?"

"First," He caught both her hands in one if his, "I *am* mad. Second, I didn't want to be on the wall. And, third, I can just walk back up." His eyes shown over the gold mask back on his face.

Perhaps he was much like the jabberwock, and if she kept looking at him, he wouldn't stop looking back.

"Thank you." It was all she could muster with blood on her clothes and five people staring at her.

"Bleah."

Lam twisted to see Wesley holding Rudyard up and staring at her with morose expression.

"The romantic tension is far too great in here for me." He

hoisted Rudyard higher and started to limp to the door in the opposite wall.

"Wait—" Rudyard twisted to Ember, "Are you—"

"She's fine! Also, *I'm* fine—your teammate, remember?"

The two bickered all the way out the door and into a darkly lit hall. Lam's eyes fell on Ember and her sister. The younger didn't even spare a nod as she started for the door, but Ember bowed slightly and said, "Thank you both. I don't know how much longer we could have gone."

Lam smiled and gripped the joker's hand. "I'm glad we could help."

Ducking her head, the princess followed the others into the hall.

"Well..." The joker reached for his weapon, retracting it as soon as it touched his free hand.

Fire lit in the jabberwock's eye sockets.

"... Now we run."

Lam was sprinting, blood on her skin, something akin to a dragon chasing her, and laughing through it all.

Her feet fell from stone to glass and Lam blinked to find her own eyes staring back at her from all sides. The joker moved beside her...and above...and beyond. It was so disconcerting but still, she pressed onwards. Hands trailing either wall, she tried to find a space where their faces didn't show in the mirrors. The hard part came when she found two.

"I think it's your turn to pick."

The joker straightened and walked into the left tunnel. Lam moved to follow, when a mirror opened behind her and a hand grabbed her mouth.

"If you call out, I will slit your tongue." The voice was light and familiar, cruel in its comfort. Once the Princess of White Chess was sure Lam wouldn't call out, she turned Lam to face her. Her light blue eyes roved over the younger princess with obvious disgust, "Rooks, why does he want you?"

Bile rose in Lam's throat, but was cut off when Adelyn shoved something hard into her hand. "Another gift from my brother."

"I don't want anything from him."

Anger turned the sky blue of her eyes to ice. "And I want you begging for mercy for the insult you dealt my family, but we don't all get what we want." She shoved Lam hard in the chest as she disappeared back down her secret tunnel. The passage seemed like cheating...but so did walking on the wall.

"Lam, what's wrong?" The joker's voice was distant but coming closer.

Lam opened her hand to find a key, the white of dried bone. "Nothing." It fell to the glass with a sharp click as she ran after the joker.

His hand landed heavily on her shoulder as she tried to walk past. "Stop running away from me."

"I've never run away from you."

Purple shrank his pupils before the iris lightened to lilac. "You have, but...just tell me what's wrong."

Lam mentally added that to her list of things she would ask about tomorrow, before sighing and slowly walking forwards. "I got a gift from another player."

"Who? When? From where? Did it hurt you? How ”

Lam slapped her hands over her ears. "Enough questions." With her eyes shut and only his touch guiding her, she had time to think. "It was Adelyn, the Princess of White Chess. She gave me a key before disappearing through a tunnel hidden behind the mirrors."

"What?" The joker stopped and stared at her with wide eyes. "Why? What the—" he cut himself off and started reaching for the walls, "There are tunnels?"

"I—" Lam froze at the realization. "I didn't think about that. That was pretty stupid of me."

"Near sighted." His hands traced the base of the wall. "Not stupid." Something clicked under his fingers and a panel popped out, bonking him in the head. He looked up with his skeletal grin. "I guess that's why Hatter thought we were good for each other."

Lam smiled as she walked into the pitch dark behind him. "How so?"

"You're the one who will jump off a cliff..."

Torches lit as Lam stepped into empty space and Cheshire caught her hands from the other side of the small hole.

"And I catch you before you hit the bottom."

Lam moved over to his side, her body pressed to his. "Very valiant of you." She twisted her hands so her fingers were laced with his.

He leaned so his mask was almost touching her lips. "It's my job."

"Even more valiant." Lam snorted before circling so his back was to the hole. "Now..." Her fingers rose from his. "You have to catch up to me to catch me." Her skirts flared out around her as she turned to run.

"See? I told you, you're always running away from me."

THE TUNNELS WERE A MAZE, but Lam happened to be very fond of mazes. She ran and laughed and sometimes shouted, when blades poked from the wall or spikes scratched her arms. Everything was cast in the orange glow of the torches, bringing a drowsy dream-like feeling to her.

Every time she thought she'd finally run fast enough, or

randomly enough, the joker would tap her on the shoulder or blow in her ear or just call out, "Are you slowing down for me, Princess? I take that as an insult."

And then Lam would grin and shoot off so that the chase could begin again.

It was…wonderful.

For miles, it seemed they ran like that. At times they would have to double back, or the floor would start to drop out, or the path would grow crushingly small, but, overall, it was painfully easy. After no more than an hour they came to a room, covered in mushrooms and vines. In the center at the back, stood a bone white statue holding two swords.

As they entered, its eyes opened and glowed.

"Lamprocapnos and Cheshire." Its voice was as harsh and old as its worn stone. "This is a game of teams, a game of alliances, a game of trust." The bright forest green of its eyes stayed fixed on the space between them. "Now, to prove your connection, you must each tell me the others' greatest fear… and why."

No.

No, no, no. Not this, not now.

It was loud in her head, the thing she loathed being called, the thing he'd called her. A parting of lips, the open syllable followed by such a crushing title. It all hurt—his hand on her arm, the shattered tea cup on the ground, every-thing tasting as sour as burned leaves.

She couldn't look, couldn't think, for if she thought on it she'd be back there, with his hand in her hair and anger burning a hole in whatever kind of heart he had. Instead, she stared at the small key hole in between the swords, seeming to taunt her with its dark eye.

She hated him, she hated him, she hated him. But she hated the idea of the joker knowing almost as much. For the grand protector and peace keeper would not like that she had put her happiness over her wisdom.

"The Prince of White Chess."

Tears stung at her eyes as she stared blankly at the joker.

"She was betrothed to him as a child."

And there it was, as clear as the white ink on black paper that he'd sent her.

"But he was vicious and sadistic."

A defense? From someone who knew? Someone who wasn't her brother or father or mother? Tears slipped from between her lashes as she stared at a boy she didn't know at all.

His eyes moved from the statue to her. "She was brave enough to put her safety above the desires of a king." Purple shown in his gaze, but it was so vastly different from the prince's.

"And Lamprocapnos, do you know Cheshire's greatest fear and why?"

"No."

The statue went still and the joker began to move to her, ready to catch her again.

"But—"

The joker and the air froze and watched.

"I would like to know, no sooner and no later than when he wants to tell me."

Lam had seen many wondrous things—she'd seen flowers open and the sun set, she'd seen swans take flight and snakes shed their skin, but nothing compared to this.

Blackness, not of anger, but a pure pupil filled his eyes to the edge of his iris, as his face turned a warm shade of rose. Even his hair seemed to rise, as if his powers were trying to escape though his skin and now open mouth.

What she had done was stupid, in theory, but Wonderland was not a place for theory and the joker was not ready to question her as the statue lowered and revealed the door.

Grinning, and wiping her eyes, Lam placed one finger under his jaw. "Well now, if you keep gawking at me like that, I might start to think you're in love with me."

And with all the strength in her pointer finger, she snapped his mouth shut, before skipping through the door. Her feet stomped once, twice, into the bright sun before cheers erupted all around.

FOURTEEN

She looked up at the scoreboard that shimmered with rankings. There they were, Lamprocapnos S. Heart and Cheshire C. Cheshire at the top, with a large lead.

"Look at the—"

"First contestants!"

"They are—"

"Two of the highest scoring-"

"Players—"

"Ever!"

"And Lamprocapnos—"

"Only sixteen!"

"Quite extraordinary."

The words of the Tweedles only twisted Lam's stomach. Her feet stumbled, but her quick recovery only led to more praise from the twins. Two nurseturtiums ran over, their green skin and petal hair shinning in the late sunlight.

"Contestant," one said, "please let us see to your wounds."

Lam could do little more than nod, her eyes on the other that approached the joker. The nurseturtiums had always fascinated Lam. They were from the Forest and filled with the power of it, but their magic didn't lessen when they were away from it.

One leaf-veined hand grazed Lam's arm, healing the small cuts, leaving nothing but a slight green hue. Her eyes rose to the much taller girl's. The nurseturtium gave a half smile as she healed a cut on Lam's ear she didn't even know she had.

"You were excellent today, and you worked well with our fellow."

"Fellow?"

"Every one from the Forest is a fellow life." Her eyes flicked to the other nurseturtium, now handing the joker a glass jar full of syrup. "Most of us know him from the times we've gone back home for festivals and celebrations."

Lam, too, watched the joker start to drink the liquid sugar as his small cuts from the glass ceiling were healed and any shards removed.

A horn sounded again, farther down the wall, and Lam turned to see Adelyn and Teon trudge out of a door, raising cheers from the Chess stands. Another pair of nurseturtiums rushed over to them and immediately started tending to a burn on Teon's arm and a cut that ran the length of Adelyn's calf.

The two princesses' eyes met over the field and Lam let herself grin and mouth, 'And I didn't even use it.'

The Princess of White Chess kept her face neutral even as her eyes shown with murder.

Before the two could do more, the horn blew yet again, and Aldwin stumbled out, holding Myla in his arms, and blinking at the cheers. Blood, a frightening amount of it, already soaked Myla's front from a cut on her neck and the Prince of Clover was dripping blood from his hands. Pain was stark on his face, but it was directed towards Myla as three nurseturtiums ran over and she was lowered to the grass.

Lam didn't pause to think as she ran. What had happened? How long had Myla been hurt? What or who had done this?

"That sadistic, scheming, son of stone!" Aldwin's eyes were round and teeth bared as he smoothed Myla's hair from her face. Glancing up, he caught sight of Teon and lunged. "You! Why in Underland did you—"

Lam grabbed the prince's arm before he could get any closer to Teon. "Aldwin! Calm down."

It was scary to see the most level-headed of the princes losing his composure in front of everyone.

He whirled on Lam. "You weren't there, you didn't see him almost slit Myla's throat."

The stands had gone silent, even though they were too far to hear what he was saying. Still, the way the Knight of White Chess turned away was cold enough to make every member of the Deck shudder.

It was a long while before the horns rang again and the silence was made even more complete as everyone waited to see if the Three of Clovers would live. Lam held the girl's hand as Aldwin sat on her other side and a nurseturtium ran her hands over Myla's neck and mouth. The other medics had their hands on her arms and either side of her hips.

"What are you doing for her?"

"Increasing blood production. In her state, it's all we can do for her."

Lam thought the horns sounded softer when they rang out, heralding the arrival of her brother and Wesley. Both were greeted by cheers and nurseturtiums, but their eyes went to their fellow prince and the three, not minding their own serious injuries. Already, some of Myla's usually faint color was back, and she was breathing more steadily as well.

The horn sounded for Ravenel and his sister, the Princess of Spades, who looked around with a calm air, accentuated by their lack of wounds. Lam met Princess Ravine's eyes and her friend opened her mouth to say something before the horn blew twice, almost at the same time, right before the sun fell behind the rolling hills of Hearts. The Princesses of Red Chess and two people Lam didn't recognize came from doors on either side of her.

The twilight was soothing as the spectators were allowed to leave the stands and find their children, siblings, and friends now released from the maze. Only the nobles could attend the first two games and most of them still had relatives competing.

"Are you alright, beautiful?" Lam's mother seemed to have appeared before her. Reaching out, she cupped Lam's cheeks and inspected her. "Hearts, I wish they didn't have to make the games so dangerous." She kissed Lam's forehead before looking over at Rudyard. "He's the one I'm most worried about."

Rudyard was talking to their father as he leaned on Wesley, who was excitedly chatting with all his sisters.

"He looks half torn apart, but Wesley has barely a scratch." The queen shook her head. "He's a leader like his father, but they never think of themselves." Her amber-red eyes turned back on Lam. "I'm glad you can protect yourself and had such a good teammate on such short notice."

Lam glanced over at the joker, now standing alone and looking off in the direction the Forest lay. "Yes. I was rather lucky." Taking one step over, Lam reached out her hand, eyes still on his back. "I think my mother has something to tell you."

He spun around with pink, and orange, and a touch of purple in his eyes before he saw the smiling faces of Lam and her mother.

"Thank you for keeping my daughter safe." The queen looked behind her to the king. "My husband would surely say the same thing, but he is a little preoccupied with our son, who I should also check on, if you don't mind." Her hands fell from Lam as she made a half bow to the joker, before walking over to Rudyard.

"And thank you, from me." Lam's hand reached for him again and this time, he reached back. Her smile turned sly as she stepped closer again. "For everything you're going to tell me tomorrow."

He rolled his eyes in an overly exaggerated way. "I was hoping you'd forget about that."

"Not a chance." Letting her exhaustion take hold, Lam slumped onto him.

"Hey, you know I'm tired, too."

"Then you can lean on me."

He grumbled something but didn't push her away as the stars began to peek their heads out from the twilight.

FIFTEEN

When they finally did get back to the castle, it was fully dark. Lam showered, cleaned her teeth, got into her night clothes, and picked up the tea that a maid had prepared for her. It was everything that she would do the nights that she got the best sleep. Stepping out onto her balcony, she could feel the warmth seeping out of the mug as the cool air brushed her face. Below her were the bleeding hearts. They seemed to glow in the moonlight.

"You forgot this."

"Or maybe I knew you'd bring it." A week ago she would have screamed to hear a voice on her balcony.

"Fair enough." The joker held out the glass vial, letting it appear before he, too, became visible.

Lam took the vial, twisting it in her hands. "Do you think it will work?"

"I hope so." He placed his now free hand on the railing.

Lam looked out over the maze that she had grown up in, so very different from the one she'd fought through that day. "Do you think that he *wanted* to be that way?" She hoped he understood she was talking about the Storyteller.

"No."

"How can you be so sure?" Lam looked over at the joker, who was also gazing at the maze.

"He doesn't have a heart." He turned to look at her, "You can't lose your heart. You can only give it to someone else."

Both of them were silent for a while, looking over the kingdom called Hearts.

"Have you ever met someone without a heart?"

He gave her a smile, something sad and wry. "Yes. You've met them too."

Lam was surprised, but felt like it wasn't her place to ask.

The joker turned so his back was against the railing and leaned backward. "It's not as bad as you think. People give away their hearts all the time...not just at weddings."

"But what if the person doesn't give theirs in return?"

Laughing, he leaned closer to her. "Well, my dear, then you have every romantic fool and half the boys in Wonderland."

Lam grabbed the rail right next to his arm. "But how do they get it back?"

"They can't." He shrugged and stared at the door of her balcony. "If they're lucky, they'll fall in love with someone else so much that their heart is transferred to that person." His eyes held something dark and he just stood there a moment. "Well...you could cut your heart out of their chest."

A chill ran down Lam's spine. "But you would have to kill them..."

The joker gave her a painful smile, the space between his teeth forming stitches over an old wound that refused to heal. "Or they would have to already be dead. I've..." His eyes grew bright purple before fading to black. "I've seen it done...once."

They stood in silence a moment, and Lam desperately

tried to think of a way to break it. The image of Teon coolly turning from Myla filled her mind.

"What kind of heart does Teon have?"

The joker gave her an appraising look as he hummed. "Teon has a heart of stone: strong, powerful, always remembering. If it's broken, that damage is there to stay."

"Oh." Lam didn't know how this would change the way that she treated him, but felt her question had changed the way the joker stood.

"Ember was well named." He went on, as if she had asked for more. Or perhaps, it was his way of breaking the silence. "She has a heart of fire: it can be strong and bright or just warm coals. Aldwin's heart is a lamp: warm but contained; something you wouldn't notice until it's gone. Myla seems to have a moth heart: fast, light, but too easily crushed. I think that she can also read hearts."

Lam grinned into the dark. "So that's why she likes Aldwin?"

"You can't blame it all on hearts, but I do think that played a part."

"And Ravenel? And Ravine?"

The joker frowned. "They're hard to tell. I know that most royal families pass down one type of heart, but theirs I don't understand." His eyes traced her doorway as he went on, "As for the younger Princess of Red Chess, Elfin, she had a heart of water like me, but right now it's snow."

"And the other two in the final game?"

He shook his head. "Not enough time, never met them before. But the Princess of White Chess has a heart of steel, like all the Royals of White Chess."

Lam shivered at the knowledge of what kind of heart the prince had and quickly shifted her attention. "And Rudyard?"

"Honey. Hearts is the only kingdom that doesn't pass down one heart type."

"Does…" Lam felt her eyes grow heavy.

The joker looked over, surprised. "Oh, I'm sorry, you should get to bed."

Nodding, Lam walked back into her room. Everything seemed like a Blood Weavers' illusion, too beautiful to be real: the soft curtains around her red sheets, her things set in their proper place, the glass bottle filled with gold liquid in her hands.

"How much do we take?"

"Don't you remember?" He sounded shocked, almost dismayed. "Hatter told us."

Lam looked up at him, drowsily. "I guess you will have to remind me."

"Three drops." The joker's gaze skidded from her eyes to her lips. "That's all."

"That's all?" A smile twitched at the corner of her mouth. "You sound almost disappointed."

"I am." His eyes were cold as he stared at the vial now in his hands. "It seems so uselessly small…"

Lam hummed and blinked. "Maybe you should just think of how potent it is."

His face softened and his shoulders dropped. "That is a much nicer way of thinking about things." Closing his hand around his bottle, he turned from her as she crawled under her sheets, settled into a comfortable position, and set the vial on her nightstand.

The joker looked back only once, but it was enough to meet her eyes. She closed them swiftly turning away so that he couldn't guess what she was thinking again. It was an impossible silly thing to want him to stay in her room and Lam didn't like feeling silly.

So she slowed her breathing and closed her eyes. Once before she had been caught between what she should and what she wanted. She wouldn't choose herself again.

CHAPTER

SIXTEEN

Everything was light in Lam's dream. Everything tasted sweet and not quite real. Everything was almost perfect. It clung to her as she woke. Keeping her eyelids shut long after her mind began taking in her breathing and the feel of her sheets.

The day before came back in a swirl of colors and touches: the white room, the joker's hand on the book, her catching him in the red crow room, walking on the wall, his hands holding her. Had she really done all of that, all the day before? And that hadn't even been the morning. Her mind sped through the ride back from the Forest and her nightmare.

Something shifted and, suddenly, laying down became strangely uncomfortable, the spell sleep had woven breaking as she opened her eyes. It was rare for her to wake early, at least by her standards. She usually rose around nine, but the sky indicated closer to seven.

Her bleary gaze went from her old chest of toys to the collection of cards in her writing desk and up to her door. She turned back to her window and balcony before she was struck by the sight of her rocking chair. In the corner between her bed and the glass door, sat her chair, upholstered with a pattern of foxes and bleeding hearts, now hosting a person.

His limbs were stretched out, one black shoe pressed the base of her nightstand. He'd removed his tie and set it on the small table, leaving his throat bare and his top two buttons undone. Red was not the joker's best color, but Lam couldn't deny that he looked effortlessly exquisite with his shoulders relaxed and head tilted to one side. Even his hair had fallen over his face, creating a curtain that half hid his closed eyes.

The middle finger of his right hand twitched and Lam held her breath. He would wake eventually, but for some reason Lam wanted him to sleep for a little longer.

Wait—

Why did she want him to sleep at all?! He was in her room, and it appeared he'd been in there the entire night. Sitting up, Lam looked down at herself and found that one side of her nightgown had fallen past her shoulder, showing a little too much skin. She lifted it back onto her shoulder and looked back to the joker.

This time, open eyes greeted her, still swirling with blissful gold and bleary blue.

"Were you watching me sleep?"

"No, I was sleeping while I was supposed to keep watch." He sat forwards and shook out his head. "It was meant to be for only an hour."

Lam gripped her hands into fists around the blankets. She always felt better with something in her hands. "Under whose orders?"

"The king's."

She was taken aback at his reticence to give her information. "Which king?"

He stood and began to walk to her bathroom. "The only king who has power in this castle."

"Why are you telling me this?"

He stopped at the sink, still in full view. "You said you wanted to know more about me." His hand went to a watch she hadn't noticed on his wrist. "I said you could have today." Setting the watch down on the counter, the joker turned on the tap and began to splash cold water on his face.

Lam was feeling oddly giddy, her body twisting inside her. "Can I ask you anything?"

He lifted his dripping head and stared at her in the reflection. "Sure." A grin slid onto his face as he turned to her and grabbed up the hand towel. "I won't promise I'll answer."

"Will you promise to try?"

"Try?" He leaned one shoulder on the door frame, dreams still hidden in the corner of his eyes.

"Try and tell me as much as you're comfortable with. Like, don't hide anything just for fun."

He ran the cloth over his face before setting it back down. "I was going to do that anyway."

He seemed different than before, different standing in her room and using her things. It felt so strange to see him go about his morning as he would in his own. Blood filled her cheeks as she realized it was so much more personal than just how he would do it in his own space. It was hers—*her* things in *her* order.

Turning to something in the bathroom she couldn't see, he held up a hand as if to stop her. "But first, I'd like to take a shower, if possible."

"Why did you splash your face if you're just going to take a shower?"

"Well," his brows rose as his eyes flicked back to her, "I was waking myself up. Now that I am awake, I realize that I feel disgusting and would like to clean my body."

Lam tucked her legs up and rested her chin on her knee. "You can if you want, but I don't have any clothes for you."

"That's fine, Hatter has some stuff that fits me." He unbuttoned his vest as he spoke.

"And you want me to get it?" Lam was not accustomed to running around, grabbing other people's things.

"Yes." Then he started walking to the door. "But I would never send a princess to run my errands."

THE JOKER RETURNED HOLDING an armful of clothes that he took to the bathroom without sparing even a nod for her. His posture was slightly stiff and his face was slightly red, leading Lam to guess Hatter had made some very pointed comments.

In five minutes—Lam knew this from the pocket watch she grabbed after putting on a day dress—the Joker emerged from the bathroom. His eyes were blue and green, matching his still wet hair, contrasting with the brown shirt he now wore, hanging loose over black pants. For once, Lam didn't just look at his expression or his eyes as he sat back down in her rocking chair. She just saw his face.

His nose was slightly flat, not up-turned like hers, nor bridged like the Hatters, or even thin and straight like her brother and father. His eyelids didn't hood when they opened. His lips were less full than hers and her family's, but they weren't exactly thin. His had a gentle bow at the top, so different from the sharp points of hers.

"What are you looking at?"

Lam watched his tongue and teeth as he spoke, mapping the sharp points and smooth muscle. "You."

"And who am I to you?"

Lam's eyes snapped up to his. "I'm the one asking questions today." She pulled the curtains back and sat down, facing him. "And I'd like to start with: How does everyone in the castle know you?"

He propped his legs up on her nightstand, smoothly missing her calendar. "Can't answer that, and, before you get mad, I quite literally can't answer it. All I can say is that it has something to do with something I've done as a joker."

"Then tell me about what you need from me."

Anger flashed over his face. "No."

"Tell me why you've had nightmares every night."

"No, I—"

"Are you going to tell me anything at all?!" Lam scrunched her legs up and wrapped her arms around them.

"I..." His face fell into something truly sorry and he didn't speak for a little while. "I was born and raised in the Forest, I had an older brother that I no longer see and have a little brother you met. When I was young, Hare would teach my brother, and eventually me, how to fight in every single way. I could fight with a needle if it was all I had and Hare acted like it would be someday. I also made a friend. He was a rath named Shaw."

It took Lam a moment to remember what rath were, but the image of the small humanoid rat people came to her.

"Well, eventually he went away and then my older brother left. After that, I spent every day working with Hare. I was still happy, I still had the oldest Cheshire and then Shire. I was eating well and sleeping well, despite the nightmares." His eyes rolled up to the ceiling and he stared at the little gold stars Lam had hung from the top of her bed canopy. "Everything really changed when I became a joker. I was...I think... fifteen? I just know I was the youngest. After that, I was assigned a mission and have lived in Cards ever since." Sitting up, he gave a half smile. "That's the overview."

Lam tilted her head so her cheek was on her knees. "What about love?"

The smile that had been so genuine slipped off his face. "What do you mean?"

"Like, crushes? Fancying someone? Did you ever sneak out to go sing poetry at your love's window?"

Both of them grinned at the idea of that, but the joker shook his head. "Romance has never been a big part of my life."

"Have you never even kissed someone?"

"Have you kissed someone?"

It was bitter on her lips, his teeth venomous, leaving her lips bleeding as he smiled.

The joker averted his attention and muttered, "Never mind, I shouldn't have asked."

There was only ever one person a betrothed girl could kiss, and, for Lam, that was her monster. She let out a sigh, a breath, anything to break the silence.

"If you really want to know, I've kissed three people."

Blinking in surprise, Lam took in the slight embarrassment with which the joker now held himself. "Go on."

He glared at her, but did as he was bid. "The first was when I was fourteen. I was at the Spring Festival that's held every year in the Forest. I was sad and angry at the time and so was she. Somehow that ended with us kissing right below her nest."

"Her nest?"

"Yes, she was a soulser, a person who guides lost souls down to Underland. They live in trees and call their homes nests." He shrugged. "Like a lot of people in the Forest, she's almost human looking, except for the second set of arms."

"She had four arms?!" His life was sounding stranger and stranger.

"Yes, it's not that odd."

"It's very odd!" But she was beaming as she said it.

The joker somehow managed to smirk and frown at the same time. "Either way, that was the first person I ever kissed." Looking back up at the ceiling, he organized his thoughts and avoided Lam's gaze. "Then there was the time at the Fall Festival…"

"Did you only ever kiss people at festivals?"

"Those were the only times I really left my house other than to see Hare." With a cough, he cleared his throat and continued, "I will be the first to admit I was drunk that time. It takes a lot of alcohol to make me even tipsy but there was a special kind of mead there…" His voice was almost wistful. "So, with my tassels in hand and honey heat in my chest—"

"Wait, tassels?" Lam lowered her knees and pulled her feet next to her. "What do you mean?"

He hummed for a moment. "Right, you don't do that in the Kingdoms… Well, tassels are similar to asking someone to dance. Each person has their own color and style, seeing as it was handmade by them. So every time you want to dance with someone, you would either put it around their neck or, if they had hair, tie it into their hair. I clearly have hair and so did she…" He paused a moment. "Well, actually I don't know if she was a *she*… Do trees even have genders?"

"You danced with a tree?"

"Tree spirt, anyway, she looked feminine. So we both tied our tassels into one another's hair and—"

"How old were you?"

"Are you going to interrupt me every few seconds?"

A sheepish grin masked her face as Lam threw up her hands. "You've interrupted yourself almost as much."

He hummed, but didn't deny it. "Anyway, I was sixteen and I danced with her for almost an hour before we fell into a bush. If I'm being completely honest, she kissed me. I just didn't do much about it."

Now it was Lam's turn to hum, though hers was far more pointed.

The joker rolled his eyes as he began the last story. "And then there was at the Summer Solstice when I was seventeen. I don't even think this one should count, seeing as I was blindfolded."

Lam made a surprised movement but didn't interrupt again.

"We were playing the age old Summer Solstice game of Sun-kissed, where one person stands in the middle and is the blindfolded sun and everyone else must take three turns around the sun before letting the next person do the same. When the music stops, the person walking around the sun must kiss them." He grinned at the memory of the strange game. "Well, the music stopped and this willowy girl grabbed my face and kissed me so hard she punctured my upper lip with her serrated teeth."

"What!" Lam felt completely justified in her outburst. "Did it leave a scar?"

"I think so."

Lam stared at his mouth, but she was sitting too far away to see anything distinct. Her eyes traveled to his brow and then up to his forehead where he had a small scar in the shape of a crescent moon.

"How did you get that scar?"

"Fighting with my brother." His voice was oddly tight and his eyes dropped into their subdued shades.

"The one that left?"

"He was the only one I fought with."

Lam looked to his arms, bare under the short sleeves of

the shirt. Scars littered his skin, taking the bronze and pulling it till it shown.

"How many scars do you have in total?"

"Fifty-seven, last time I counted."

Lam's eyes grew wide at the number. That was more weeks than there were in a year. That was more then the number of cards in a deck. "Will you tell me about them?"

"All of them?"

"Well, I don't really have any other plans for today."

CHAPTER

SEVENTEEN

L am had never listened to one person for so long. She couldn't sit still the entire time, so she played solitaire as he told her about his scars, one by one. He started with a scar he had on his abdomen that he didn't bother showing her and continued down his back and arms before ending up at his legs.

Servants came and brought food, the sun peaked and fell, and when it grew dark, Lam sipped on tea as she turned on all her lamps. Her cards were shuffled again and again and laid in their seven stacks over and over. It was another thing Lam wished she could live in forever, her sitting on the sheepskin rug and the joker leaning forwards and telling her of his strange, wondrous life.

Some things he couldn't say, simply skimming over the scars he got while acting as a joker. Some of them were too painful to go into detail, but at others he would grin, excitedly pointing at the spot on his elbow, or neck, or foot. Lam had never imagined how full life in the Forest was. He'd been more places, seen more things, and talked to far more people than Lam, despite his rather secluded lifestyle. Even when

Lam got to see those things, it was at a distance, and most of the people she met were nobles.

Her hands picked up the jack of diamonds and placed him on the queen of spades as the joker told her of one on his heel.

"So I was playing hazard with some Blood Weavers—"

Lam's eyes flicked up from the eight of hearts she'd just flipped over. "There are still Blood Weavers!" She had always been taught they had all been hunted by the men and wolves from Red Chess.

The joker nodded, almost excitedly. "Sure! Most of them were driven from their native homes in White Chess when the two Kingdoms formed the Board, but plenty still live in small villages in the Forest. Though, their power is far weaker than the elder Weavers and they can't do as many complex things outside of White Chess." He waved his hand as he propped his foot on his other knee. "Anyway, I was playing hazard with these Weavers and they were feeling lucky, so they asked me to make a deal with them." His eyes roved over Lam's cards. "Deals are very important in the Forest and once made, whether or not you're magically bound, you follow through. Also, you can put that eight on the nine of clovers over there."

"I know." Lam couldn't help grinning as she moved the card.

"So they asked me what I would have from them. I asked if they could heal any wound, and they said they might..." He paused, smile frozen on his face. "Well," picking at the scar, he looked back at his foot, "they couldn't heal the wound, so I asked if they could fill one of my vials full of their blood."

"What were you going to do with Blood Weaver's blood?"

"Give it to Hare! He said he always wanted to work with it in his potions. Anywho, they accepted as long as I would give them my skin if they won."

"All of it?"

"I'm sure that's what they were thinking." He shrugged and sat back. "One of them lost the first round and gave up a vial of their blood. In the next round, both the second Weaver and I threw out, meaning we both lost, so I got another vial of blood. Then I took out my knife, cut off my feet calluses, and gave it to them."

Lam moved her king of hearts into the empty space left by the eight. "Why would you cut off all of your calluses?"

"Everyone in the forest has made one bad deal or another and I didn't want to make them feel worse than they did."

Lam snorted as she put a ten of clovers on the jack of hearts that had just appeared. "I bet it hurt a lot more to get back all those calluses than it did to heal a small cut for draining blood."

Rocking himself, the joker sighed. "It did hurt, but it was fun as well."

"You have an odd definition of fun."

"Says the person who's been playing solitaire for the past ten hours."

"I was listening to you!"

He smiled down at her as she swept up the game she'd won with only a tiny bit of cheating. "Why do you bother cheating if you're just playing against yourself?"

"Because I'm playing against chance, not myself."

He tilted his head and studied her—the way her thick red curls fell around her face, the darkness of her freckles against her rosy cheeks. Even her hands were fascinating, with their thin fingers that hid so much strength.

Lam tapped the deck of cards into their box, closed it, set it aside, and stretched. "What was the game you played?"

"Hazard?"

"That one. I've never played it."

"How have you, a princess of Cards, never played hazard?"

Lam rolled out her shoulders. Perhaps she had played solitaire for too long. "Well it's not a card game, is it? Why should I know it?"

"Because it's a vital game in Forest culture!"

"I hate to be the bearer of terrible news, but I was never really taught about the Forest."

He grumbled something as he stood from the chair and looked around. "Do you have dice?"

"Maybe."

"You're not even sure if you have dice?" His shock and hurt were only exaggerated. "How do you not have one of the symbols of the Forest?"

Lam didn't bother answering as she went to her writing desk and searched for the set of dice she'd gotten when she was ten. She pulled it out in all its glory: six gold and scarlet dice, neatly packaged in an ornate box.

She turned around to find the joker wearing a dubious expression. "Now that is not a symbol of the Forest."

"Well, it's what I have."

Stepping over, he took the box from her hands, opening it and taking one out. "Are they actually even?" He threw it up and let it fall in his hand several times before nodding. "Even enough. The embossing makes it a little unfair, but that shouldn't affect us too much." He pulled another out and moved to sit down on a space not covered in rugs. "We only need two, so you can put the rest back."

Closing the box, Lam set it in her desk and walked over. "How did you do that?"

"Do what?"

"Test it? How could you feel if it was weighted?"

A smirk pulled at his mouth. "Believe it or not, I was born

like that. I always know the balancing point of anything. If I feel every side of the die, I can know if it's weighted." He turned back to his hand where he was twisting the gold dice over each other. "Once I feel that something is off, it's easy to tell where it's coming from."

He held one up for Lam to look at as she sat down. "If you were going to weigh a die, you would weigh it off center, either by using another metal or leaving a pocket of air." He set the die next to the other. "That's why, in Forest competitions, every die is carved from wood right there in front of everyone and tested by someone like me, who's blindfolded and not told who's playing the game."

"Your people seem to rather enjoy blindfolds."

"We used to blindfold humans for sport a long time ago."

"You what!?"

He laughed, a sweet and slightly damaged sound, not at all like how she'd imagined his laugh. "We wouldn't hunt them or anything. We'd just blindfold them and grant them one wish if they could find us."

"Hmm. I would have let you blindfold me." Lam stared at the dice going around in the joker's hand.

His head flicked up, eyes bright orange. "What?"

"I can move around pretty well in the dark and I know how you walk now."

The orange faded to a curious green as he leaned closer to her. "Really? How do I walk?"

"Unevenly," Lam snorted. "It feels like you're tripping all over the place even when you're going in a straight line."

"It feels?"

Lam glanced at her hands. "Yes. I don't really hear it...or see it, but I can *feel* you next to me." Scooting back, she held up her hands. "Here, I'll show you what I mean." She closed her eyes and let out a breath. A gold energy filled her mind, reconstructing the room she sat in with faint lines. The warm color of the joker was the strongest, cutting his form away from the rest world.

"Here are your eyes." Lam leaned forwards and brushed his lashes, so barely missing his eyes. "And your nose." Lam laid her fingers on it for a moment before moving on. "And your mouth." Her hand slipped over his lips, one of her fingernails catching for half a second. Blushing, she leaned even closer, laying her hands flat over his chest. "And here's your heart!" But... it felt cold, and painful, and like something she shouldn't feel.

She pulled her hands back and opened her eyes at the same time. His eyes were...wet, purple softened by the tears that waited to fall. Turning his head, he leaned forward and laughed, but it wasn't the jagged, gentle, beautiful laugh of earlier.

"That's a pretty good skill." He was quiet for a beat before handing her the dice. "Now, let me teach you a new game."

"And that's another round to Cheshire!" the joker crowed.

Lam glared at the dice showing twelve. "I don't think I like this game very much."

"I think you don't like losing."

"Who likes losing?" she asked, handing him the dice.

He shook them in his hands. "I sometimes like losing. As long as the game was fun, it doesn't really matter to me." He closed his eyes and stilled the dice in his hands. "I'm calling main on... seven."

Opening one eye, he shook the dice and spilled them onto the hard wood. Seven dots stared up at them.

"You're cheating!"

"How could I be cheating? I bet something different each time."

Lam puffed out her cheeks as she fought to find an answer.

"Think of it as the opposite of solitaire. Now you're working *with* chance."

Lam swept up the dice and shook them hard in her hands. "I don't think I like chance very much. And I'll main six."

The joker grinned as eleven spilled out. "And I think chance doesn't like you very much."

Lam glared at the dice, so similar to the gold that she saw sometimes, so much like the crowns she'd worn since she was born, so very reminiscent of the gold wax the Prince of White Chess used to seal his letters. "Perhaps you're right."

But chance had given her far more than it had ever taken, maybe more than it *could* take away. Her eyes rose to the ceiling and her gold stars. "But I have yet to meet tragedy face-to-face."

A knock at the door startled Lam out of her reverie as her personal maid poked her head in. "I'm sorry to disturb you, but the king and queen are asking for you to join them for dinner in the hall."

"...What?" It was rare for them to eat in the dining hall, especially when The Game was going on. But...she hadn't even checked on Rudyard and her parents were probably worried when the maids brought news that the cyan-haired boy was spending the day in her room.

Rising, Lam tucked her hair behind her ear. "Right, of course, tell them I'll be there momentarily." She turned to say goodbye to the joker, but the maid spoke again.

"Sir Cheshire, you are also urged to join."

He straightened, not meeting Lam's eyes. "Tell them I am grateful to join them this evening."

Nodding, the girl ducked out of the room, leaving an awkward silence.

"You were very polite."

"One of the many things I've learned to be as a joker." He took the first few steps forwards and Lam followed as he led the way down.

Lam was barely surprised that he knew the layout of the castle, but she was surprised he took the main staircase. It meant they entered the hall clearly side by side, as couples or siblings sometimes would.

Her gaze quickly took in her father's glower, her mothers pursed lips, and Rudyard pushing food around his silver plate. The silence between them was somehow both impatient and reflective, like a puzzle that was yet to be solved.

Lam and the joker slid into seats next to one another, Lam facing Rudyard and the joker facing an empty chair.

"What took you so long?"

"Walking." Lam didn't even bother to hide her eyebrow raise as she looked to her father. "I was only just informed that we are eating together tonight." Her eyes drifted over her brother and to the other end of the table where her mother sat. "Is something wrong?"

"If you find attempts on your brother's life as something wrong," Rudyard said, finally releasing his fork from his death grip, "I would say yes."

"Someone tried to kill you?"

Rudyard simply crossed his arms and looked to the king.

"Yes, two unnamed individuals made an attempt to stab your brother as he was recovering in his bed. They have not been identified, but we believe they are people of Chess," His eyes grew painfully wary as they met Lam's. "Most likely White Chess." His stilted words struck Lam with an all-too-familiar, suffocating feeling.

It had filled her when the prince had kissed her, his hands digging into her side. It had bled out of her mouth when he'd come to the palace after the engagement had been officially called off. It was in his white ink, in the gold seal, in the matches he lit as he walked around a maid when Lam was too scared to help. Lam felt as if she'd been thrown back into his arms, in his room, in the bloody, bleeding words he'd written to her day after day.

"It isn't your fault."

And suddenly she could breath again.

The joker laid his hand face up on the table, near her, open. But Lam couldn't take it, not when her parents were watching her, not under the eyes of glass lightbulbs or surrounded by the mouths this castle called doors.

So, instead, Lam looked up into his eyes, calm but swirling with a deadly anger on her behalf.

"You made the right choice, no matter how much it might not feel like it."

"I don't think you have the authority to say that," the king countered.

The low anger bled into his eyes. "I think I have the freedom to comfort a girl who feels like her actions almost got her brother killed."

The king sat up taller. "This wouldn't have been a problem if you'd done what I asked."

"Last I knew, I am here for the princess, not the prince."

Lam, and her confusion, jumped as her father slammed his fist into the table. "You serve me!"

"I serve Cards." Cheshire, too, straightened. "And my orders were to keep Lamprocapnos Heart safe."

"Orders?" It was the first thing out of Lam's mouth and everyone turned to her. "Whose..."

Rudyard didn't meet her eyes, her mother looked only

slightly less confused than Lam felt, and her Father was about to break his teeth by how hard he was clenching his jaw.

"Whose orders?"

Shame crept into the joker's face, unwarranted and unwelcome, but there all the same.

Steely power turned in the king's eyes as he looked at the joker. "This boy was assigned to keep you safe from the Prince of White Chess and anyone who might seek revenge for your perceived slight upon the royal family. He has been working for your safety and nothing more for the past two years."

Two years. He'd been protecting her since he was sixteen and she was fourteen. Scars, stories he'd skipped over, pain in his eyes and in his chest.

Storytellers...

"What?" It was from Lam's mother. The queen had anger in her cheeks, turning them pink. "You told me a joker was protecting her... not..." Wide eyes turned on the joker. "You are a joker."

He inclined his head slightly. "My name is Cheshire, son of Wonderland, and I am the Dark Joker."

It was silly. She knew all of this. Of course there was a better reason for him being there than.... Than what? He wanted to? He'd found her interesting at the ball and was tagging along like some stray cat? That he liked spending time with her?

Her gaze darted from the joker, to her mother, then landing on a slight green mark along the base of Rudyard's jaw that hadn't been there yesterday. Everything was getting blurry and bloody and bruised.

"I'm sorry," Lam stood and folded her hands, "I think I would like to go to my room now, if you will excuse me." Lam stepped back from the scene and the set—the table filled with food and her empty plate. Then she turned and fled up the stairs.

Water dripped from her eyes and she saw lies in every shadow.

'I can keep you safe.'

From what? she had wanted to shout, You're the thing I fear most.

The White Prince in her head chased her all the way back to her room, till the door was shut and locked and she was burrowed under her sheets. It was then that Lam feared she had made a great mistake.

While she was gone, one of the servants must have delivered her mail, a letter from the daughter of the Six of Hearts, a postcard from her non-royal grandmother, and a black envelope addressed in white ink.

To the Princess of Hearts,
my beautiful fool

EIGHTEEN

My Dear Fool,

I hope this letter finds you well. The Games have been far more exciting now that you are in them. I wish I could watch you like this every day, but, alas, I must live off of stolen glances.

I see you have made a new friend—the boy with the teal hair. I hope he doesn't worm his way into your heart. You already have so many filthy creatures burrowed into it, and I cannot stand the idea that someone would try to steal you away from me.

With impatience,
Your King.

T he words stared up at her in his swooping hand, all the eyes dotted with sharp flicks of his pen. The ink, ever waterproof, shown in neat lines even as her angry tears began to warp the page.

She was angry. Angry at her father for keeping his plans for her secret. Angry at her mother for acting like it wasn't even about her. Angry at her brother for not even being concerned they'd both been lied to. But maybe she was the only one who hadn't known. Perhaps she was sitting at the table with people all wearing masks like the Storyteller had.

Lam grabbed the top of the Prince's letter with both hands and tugged. The paper was annoyingly tough and her hands were shaking. One finger slipped and began to spill blood onto the black. Yelling, screaming in frustration and pain, Lam threw the page down and moved to her fireplace.

Logs had been set aside for her even as the weather began to warm. She lifted one of the smaller ones onto a pile of kindling already waiting. Her eyes searched for a matchbox and found it on her desk. It was gold and red, like the dice.

Storytellers, the dice, the joker, the job—it all was too sweet to taste bitter yet. But it would—everything eventually became unbearable if she held it in her mouth for too long.

The first match snapped as soon as it was in her hand. Muttering, she tossed it into the fireplace and pulled out another. She struck it against the box...and nothing happened. Again and again she struck it, but she couldn't get it to light.

'Are you scared of fire?'

No. She was better than this.

As soon as she shut her eyes, she was twelve and back in the kitchen.

'I can keep you safe.'

But sadistic joy was bright in his eyes as he covered her and pulled her from the fire he had started.

Tears blurred her view as she opened her eyes again, but the next blink sent her back into another memory.

He was stepping so lightly, his heeled shoes seemed to float, as he sang ring-around-the-rosie and dropped matches closer and closer to the young maid he circled.

She couldn't do it. No matter how fast she ran, or how strong she got, or how far she stood away from the Prince of White Chess, she could never escape his pale shadow. The match and box escaped her hands along with her air. Was she even breathing anymore? Was Wonderland simply keeping her around because it wasn't done with her? Hands—her hands—shaking and foreign, covered her ears as her legs pressed her already useless lungs. Shards of glass, shards of the world, memories of blood and false love were stabbing every piece of Lam... and she was scared of how it would end.

She thought she would hate it when he came in. Already his taste was starting to get bitter, but she couldn't help the way he made her feel: safe, and seen, and a touch revered.

"Princess."

A shiver coursed along Lam's body. He didn't say 'my' like the prince, he didn't rush the word. Though her eyes were shut and her head hidden between her knees, she felt it as he knelt before her. That strange, hollow, yet solid boy.

The joker didn't try to touch, to take her, to tame her. He sat and waited.

"Are you here to watch me cry?"

"I'm here for you." Steady and unapologetically... himself. The joker didn't always tell the truth, but he did say what he meant.

Lam raised her head even as more tears ran down her cheeks. "And who am I to you?"

"The Princess of Hearts." His eyes began to run over her freckles again, making constellations out of discolorations.

"Lam." He leaned closer to her.

"The person I would die for if that would keep her safe." Already his eyes were red, but black tongues flicked out.

"The person I'd kill for, too."

His face was so close, so honest, so different from hers, still dripping tears. With shaking hands, Lam cupped his face and ran her thumbs under his eyes and across his cheeks. They dipped to his lips and Lam pulled at them to see his teeth. Everyone had thought her an odd girl as a child, studying things most people forgot, but Lam loved to know how things worked...mostly so she could follow all the unspoken rules.

Her thumb fell into his mouth and he shivered as she ran over the points of his teeth and the gap between his canines and his second pair of teeth. Their mouths were different, shaped in different ways, his teeth weren't perfectly straight or perfectly bright, but—

"Lum."

The word was pushed aside by her fingers that she quickly withdrew. "Sorry, I just find teeth...fascinating." Was that bad?

"Teeth are very useful." He moved to sit at her side and deftly swept her into his arms and stood. "I wouldn't say I find them fascinating, but they are quite interesting."

Lam snorted again, right before he dropped her on her bed. "Now that was rather inelegant of you."

He grinned, seeming much taller now that she was laying down. "But, just look," he brushed his fingers under her eye, "you're not crying any more."

Lam's own hands shot up to her cheeks. It was true. Usually when she began to cry that hard, she would keep crying for at least an hour. As soon as the joker started to move away, Lam's hand went from her face to his arm.

"Wait!" She couldn't ask that. It would be stupid, inappropriate... "Can you hold me for a while?"

And they were both stunned by the question. Lam curled so her back was to him, pressing herself into her sheets and pillow. "Never mind."

He said nothing as he untied his shoes. Like everything, it made no sound, but the quiet was so much worse. Gingerly laying next to her, he turned his body so his chest was flush with her back. His legs came up to cradle hers and his arm fell over her waist. His head was lower than hers, breaths hot on her neck. Everything was loud inside her, from her toes to her eyes, beating like a drum. But the thing that surprised her the most...was how safe she felt.

She must've shifted slightly, because his hand fell to lay along her abdomen. Lam's gasp was short and light, but enough for the joker to pull his hand back and lay it on her shoulder instead. They stayed like that for a long time, safe but impermanent. When he finally moved to get up, Lam felt like she had missed something—something unshown and unsaid. She twisted back in time to see him pick up his shoes and the black letter. His eyes showed anger, but he shoved it in his pocket with no more fanfare. Walking over to the lamp, he smiled down at her. "I'll be right outside your door if you need anything."

Lam scooted so she was under the covers. "It must be tiring, having someone's life on your shoulders, Joker."

"Well," he played with the lamp's pull chain, "it's my life too."

"What do you mean?"

With a sharp click, the room became black. "A lot of things I shouldn't say." She felt his form move to the door but halt with his hand on the knob. "Oh, Lam, if you don't mind, I'd prefer it if you called me Cheshire."

A bit of light spilled in before he shut the door behind him. Lam rubbed her head into her pillow, pulled up her blankets, and smiled.

"Alright, Cheshire."

CHAPTER

NINETEEN

Early morning sun stabbed into Lam's eyes. Although she was sure she'd closed the curtains, there was no denying the soft heat on her face.

"Get up, sleepyhead. We're heading to the Forest."

Pushing herself to sitting, Lam blinked up at her backlit brother. "What?" It was the only word that perfectly captured her state of mind.

"You," he pointed at her with an overly dramatic swish, "me," his thumb was driven back to his chest, "Mack," he waved vaguely to the world outside her room, "Hatter," he continued to wave off into the distance, "and the joker," he poked his pointer finger at the door, "are all heading to the Forest in an hour, so…" he waved vaguely again but this time at her.

Lam let a smile tip her annoyance. Her brother only acted like this when he wanted to say he was sorry for something, but didn't really know how. Slipping from her sheets, Lam stretched and looked out her balcony window. "What time is it?"

"Time for you to keep track of your watch."

Snorting, Lam grabbed her beautiful watch from were it sat on her nightstand. "How are you feeling?"

"Fine enough." His tone was short and strong, neither open for debate or agreement.

Humming, Lam ran her finger over the watch's protective glass. Nine-thirty stared up at her in gold symbols. The second hand clicked away, but Lam's mind turned it back and ran over the night before. It still hurt, like a gash that had scabbed, something she could easily reopen if she kept picking at it. And why shouldn't she pick at it? They were the ones that had gotten the knife so close to her skin.

"Did you know?" The words were said in time with her clicking the watch closed.

"Know...what?"

Lam turned back and Rudyard raised his hands. "Fine, I know what, but I didn't know." He paused and frowned, almost amazed by the fact that such a poor sentence had come out of his mouth. "I didn't know that the joker was assigned to you or anyone. It was only yesterday that I learned that someone was keeping you safe from—" he skidded over the prince's name, "that *particular bastard*, and it was only at dinner that I learned your guard was Cheshire."

His hands fell to his sides and real regret shown in his eyes. "I was rude to you last night and I should have talked to Dad on your behalf. But I was so confused, and angry, and a little shell shocked from almost being killed... But now I would like to say I'm sorry for not standing up for you and I don't think any of this is your fault. Cheshire is right. You made the correct choice in calling off your engagement."

Tilting his head to one side, he looked out the window again. "That aside, Mom and Dad think it would be better if we stay somewhere other than in the castle before the ball.

We will finish up The Game, everything will be wonderful, and we can all have cake."

Walking forward, Lam hugged her brother. "Sounds like a plan."

～

"I can't do this anymore!"

In the uncomfortably small carriage, Lam threw her hand of cards up, "Cheshire, how much longer? It feels like it's been a lifetime!"

Cheshire, sitting across from her, grabbed her king of spades from mid-air and laid it down along with the queen and jack that had already been in his hand. Flicking his wrist, he revealed the watch strapped there and nodded. "It's only been one hour."

Lam groaned, "You're telling me we have four more hours of this?"

"Try sleeping," Rudyard said from under a blanket he'd curled up with in the corner.

"I don't want to sleep!"

Mack grabbed a card from the face down stack on the floor. "Do you want to be a little quieter?"

Huffing, Lam sat back in her seat, leaving Mack and Cheshire to finish the game of gin rummy without her. Her eyes moved from the cards in Cheshire's hands to his face.

Cheshire.

He'd always had a name, but not one that Lam had used, seen, grown attached to. Now he wasn't just *the joker*, he was Cheshire, a boy covered in scars and just as many stories.

His eyes darted red as he looked back at her, and, even as he looked away, a smile grew on his face. Cheshire. It shouldn't have felt any different, but it did. It felt like she'd left the joker on the balcony and the boy who stayed with her —who'd talked to her, who'd held her—was someone new.

"You're going to hurt your eyes if you keep staring like that."

Lam jutted out her chin. "Wouldn't you know?"

Cheshire laughed as he picked up the card Mack had just set down. "I do know, because I tend to stare like that a lot."

Lam felt the carriage drop, or maybe that was just her jaw.

Again, Cheshire laughed in his soft, jagged way. "Intently, I mean. I have to watch anyone and everyone around you."

"What about me?" Her nervous hands tucked a stray stand of hair behind her ear.

"Well, watching you is a luxury I am rarely afforded."

Rudyard sniffed loudly and Mack raised a impressed eyebrow. Lam forced herself to look out the window, but she couldn't force down her smile.

Time seemed to drag its heels on the thoroughfare from the capital of Hearts and deep into Diamonds. She hadn't watched as they rode down the streets of Hearts' capital, the Pulse, but she had seen it plenty of times.

The houses were made from rich wood imported from Spades and the Forest and local clay brought up from Hearts' own soil. Red glass shone in the windows of pubs, while small shrines to the Storytellers dotted the alleyways. Only in Spades were the Storytellers still given churches, but in every country in Wonderland you could find people who still worshiped them.

Eyes drifting to Cheshire, Lam wondered if they worshiped the Storytellers in the Forest. Looking up at her, Cheshire smiled, and Lam quickly turned back out the window.

Diamonds was very different from Hearts—craggy and

riddled with mines. There had been a period of time when Spades had tried to match the mining in Diamonds, but their natural resources were nowhere similar. In Hearts, the hills and mountains rolled with fields and grazing animals, but in Diamonds the hills didn't roll at all.

The jagged landscape slowly lulled Lam till her eyes drifted closed. Distantly, she thought of the potion in her bag, but her body was too far gone to move.

A HAND REACHED FORWARD, fingers left ungloved.

"Don't bother running."

Her eyes snapped open as the Storyteller's hand closed around her throat. His head tilted to one side, eyes digging into her from behind a smiling porcelain and gold mask, matching the beautiful, soft world around them, so opposite from his dark, ragged clothes.

"You're so much like Bunny..." He pulled Lam close as his eyes roved over her skin. "You both like to act like the victims when you've been playing the game for almost as long."

Air tried to claw its way into her, but he held her throat too tightly. Tears started to spill over her cheeks and into her gasping mouth. Letting go, the Storyteller threw her onto the ground.

"Every good story needs a villain." The words were muttered, as the boy flicked two old-fashioned throwing knives into his hands. "You have so many good options." Black metal of his left knife was brought to her cheek, then up to her her eye. "I would love—"

"Runt!"

He made a disgusted sound as he turned back to a woman. Lam noticed the five other people standing behind her, but her attention was swiftly bought back to the woman. Her skin was pale, ghostly so, and it was with a start that Lam realized the girl must have been a Blood Weaver. The slight relief Lam had felt when the woman called out was replaced with trepidation.

"What did I tell you about playing with my food?"

Lam felt the boy called Runt sneer from beyond his mask. "Only you would call a human food."

The woman reached inside her red cloak and pulled out a wood-cutting axe. "How about I just tell you to leave."

"What if I don't feel like it?" Even though he didn't stand at more than five feet, the boy went toe-to-toe with the woman. "What if I feel like leading this story?"

Harsh steel of the wood axe was brought to press under the mask. "You're always welcome to try."

The woman's red eyes flicked to Lam, sharp and unforgiving, but also wide like...a bunny. "Leave us, little Heart."

LAM SAT UP WITH A START, in time with them bumping over the bridge into the Forest. Afternoon light brought out the color of Cheshire's hair and his worried expression.

"Another nightmare?"

Shaking her head, Lam looked at the very real carriage around them—Mack mindlessly twisting a needle between his fingers and Rudyard asleep under his blanket. "...Not exactly." The world had been nothing like anything Lam had seem before. A shiver coursed over her body as tales of the Storytellers' realm ran through her mind. Had she been brought to the land of the immortal Storytellers...while she slept? The idea seemed ridiculous but...

"What is it?"

Blinking rapidly, Lam focused on Cheshire. "Nothing."

"Smooth." He leaned back and put one foot—the foot with the scar—on his knee. Lam made a face and he lifted his hands. "No, no, don't let me keep you from your secret plotting."

"I am not plotting."

A scarred finger was waved in her direction. "Tell that to your face."

"I rather like my face the way it is." She propped her elbow on her knee and her face on her hand.

Cheshire, too, moved forward. "That makes two of us."

"Ahem." The needle had stilled in Mack's hand as the corner of his mouth twitched. Lam could never tell if it was the beginnings of a smile or frown. "I know this isn't how you normally think of me, but I am still your permanent chaperone until you are married, Lam." His eyes softy slid to Cheshire. "You might not want to kiss someone right in front of me."

"I wasn't going to kiss her."

One of Mack's shoulders lifted. "We will never know."

The conversation ended there and stayed absent all the way to their destination.

"This isn't your house, is it?" The clearing that Lam stepped into was completely different than the one with Mister Willow.

Cheshire walked past her to a post with many small signs on it. They read:

'Keep Out.'

'Might Explode.'

'I am a Joker!'

'Also Mad.'

'Stay Out.'

'Unless your name is Cheshire, Hatter, or Cheshire.'

"This is Hare's." He knocked on the wood once before jumping down the hole right behind it.

Feet, waist, shoulders, and head were swallowed by the rabbit hole, and Lam couldn't help gasping and rushing over. Her knees fell to the grass and hands moved to either side of the gap in the world. "Cheshire?"

"Here!"

"Don't do that!" But her words were half a laugh as she swung her legs into the dark. Twisting back, Lam glanced over at Mack and Hatter unloading the luggage and Rudyard still blinking himself awake. Trepidation was grabbing at her skin, but it couldn't find a hold as she pushed off from the earth.

The fall took longer than Lam had expected and she fell heavily onto a pile of pillows seven feet tall. They moved to cover her, burying her in between fabric and feathers, awfully similar to one of her nightmares. Trepidation was pushed to one side as fear grabbed her by the neck and sent her thrashing.

"Lam!" A hand grabbed her, pulling her from the bedding. "What's wrong? What happened?"

"I—" Her eyes were drawn back to the brightly colored pillows as Rudyard fell on them. Shaking her head, she looked back at Cheshire. "I'm fine."

"I'm not."

Lam, Cheshire, Rudyard, and Mack—who had just landed half on Rudyard—all looked at the March Hare, tapping his foot in a furious beat. "They expect me to babysit four children!"

CHAPTER

TWENTY

"You're not *babysitting* us." Lam hadn't been taken care of like that since she was six, but her refusal did nothing for Hare's scowl.

"And that attitude is proving my point." Spinning on one heel, he walked back into the room Lam assumed he'd come from.

The four left in the hall looked around as Rudyard and Mack stood, Rudyard nursing the elbow Mack had landed on.

Hare's head emerged from the room, gold dripping from his eyes onto the floor. "Well, don't make me tell you three times."

Then his head was retracted and Lam led the way, with Rudyard grumbling, "Once would have been nice."

As soon as Lam came to the door, she felt vomit build behind her lips. Her waist bent and she clutched at the door. It was...nauseating—bottles on every shelf, in every size, spilling onto the counter, the bright lamps under mismatched shades that didn't seemed to stop the light one bit, the sink coated with layers of bright colors, the thousands of different smells.... Even the tiles of the floor seemed to twist as her eyes met it. She closed her eyes so tightly that she saw phosphenes.

"Hare..." Hatter's calm voice slid over Lam's back as he stepped past her into the room. "Give the kids some warning next time."

Foot starting up its drum again, Hare huffed. "Why? Anyone worth their blood should be able to survive seeing some bottles."

"It's not the bottles." Shakily, Lam looked up at Hare. "It's the light, and the smell, and...everything."

He moved over to her and grabbed her by the face, titling her chin up and dropping something into her eye. It felt like he'd just pressed a wad of cotton to it, but it didn't hurt. Hare pulled away before Lam could. Rolling her eyes, Lam looked around to find the world to be more bearable, at least in her left eye.

"You forgot my other eye."

Hare looked up from the bottle he was in the act of corking. "So I did." He grabbed her face and again and muttered around the cork now in his mouth, "I forgot you still had that."

"Not all of us are missing an eye, believe it or not." Rudyard called from the doorway, not daring to enter the strange room.

Letting go of Lam's face, Hare corked the bottle again. "Well, some of you have stuff to put away in your rooms."

"You haven't assigned us rooms."

"Not every piece of your life comes on a silver plate, knave. Now go and make yourself a room."

Cheshire smirked as he led Mack and the trailing prince to the rooms further down the hall.

Still blinking at the altered world around her, Lam ran her fingers over a shelf. "You're really good at making potions."

"I have been doing it for six hundred years."

Lam spun to face him.

"How old are you?!"

"Right now, thirty-two, but this is my twenty-ninth life."

She thought he had been named after the March Hare but...

"Do you remember all the things from your pasts?"

"Absolutely not. And I don't want to. If I remembered all the things from twenty-nine lives, my brain would explode. I only remember the most important things." He turned his brown eye on her as he hunched over a potion on the counter.

"Do you remember the Evil Queen of Hearts?" Lam's voice was small, and delicate, like glass shards.

"Of course." Wiping his hands, he stood to his full height, even his blank eye seeming to bore into her. "And that axe."

Flinching, Lam looked away, twisting a piece of hair behind her ear. Her voice was even smaller than it was before. "What was she like?"

"Cold." He turned and grabbed his axe, resting in one corner. "And broken."

For the first time since Lam had met him, Hare smiled. "So, nothing like you."

Lam felt like he had given her the sun to drink. She smiled up at him and walked out of the room after him. "Thank you."

"Don't thank me yet, blooderfly. Let's see how you feel after our practice session."

A LOT WORSE. That was how she felt two hours later. Her arm shook as she went through the motions again and again.

"No, no, no. Higher, you're not going for their stomach." Hare went over to her with a towel and a bottle of water.

"I need food! Not just water." Her stomach carried the statement.

"If you ever want to be a joker, you need to know how to fight and move for days on water alone. If you want to eat, you have to find your food." He gestured to the forest around them. Pausing, his mouth closed and one of his ears twitched. "Actually, that's a great idea." His eyes found Cheshire in a tree before returning to Lam. "For now, you'll work with Cheshire. He'll tell you what you can eat and what will kill you." Hare handed her the water and towel before disappearing down his rabbit hole, where everyone else was.

As she approached him, Cheshire looked down, past his pad of paper. He sat on an old oak branch and had been watching them from there as they practiced. Lam just stared up at him, too tired to say anything.

His eyes darted over her face, finding the words she couldn't say. "Oh, sure."

She was rather glad he could do that.

Jumping down, he pulled his arms over his head and stretched. "Ok, let's start with the most common things." Smiling, he pointed at a small yellow plant that Lam had seen all over the forest floor.

"That one will make you vomit for up to an hour," he flipped his hand up, "but doesn't have any lasting effects. That one," he pointed at a long vine with bright orange flowers, "will cause temporary blindness and nausea, but the blindness is only permanent if you ingest it in large amounts."

Lam was starting to feel green.

His finger moved to a small, blue flower at her feet. "That one is edible..."

A spark of hope.

"...but only the petals. The rest of it will give you tremors and hallucinations."

The spark was dimmed.

In all, after half an hour, there were only four plants that had no bad side effects, ten that you had to prepare in a special way, and fifty-eight that were poisonous.

"So, those are all the most common ones. If you see one that you don't recognize...best to leave it alone.

"Because I have so many good options already," Lam drawled, biting into one of the two edible fruits.

It had the flavor of sawdust and the texture wasn't much better. And yet the other one was worse. As she chewed, Lam realized that, once again, Cheshire had successfully distracted her.

"Thank you."

"For what?"

Lam ran her fingers over the fruit's rough skin. "For caring enough to keep distracting me."

"Believe it or not," Cheshire stepped closer to her, Lam's back already up against a tree, "I rather like distracting you."

A smile crept over her face and she lifted her chin, nose almost meeting his. "Don't you mean it's your job?"

"It can be both." He didn't move at all, his lips and tongue forming the words so softly, Lam didn't even feel it on her skin.

"For how long?"

"As long as it has to be." Turning from her, he started to walk to the rabbit hole, calling back, "Hopefully one day I won't have to do it as a job. Now, let's go see if Hare has something to eat."

Lam rushed over to him, face flushed and grin stupid. "Now look who's smoothly changing the topic."

Twisting back to her and shrugging, he grinned. "Can't help it." Then he stepped back and fell into the hole, slipping from view.

HARE DID, in fact, have something to eat. It was a large cake, baked to perfection.

"You're sure that's not the growing kind?" Hatter asked, inspecting the frosting.

"I'm twelve percent sure that it is."

Rudyard's head whipped up. "That it is the growing kind or the normal kind?"

Hare just hummed and went on cutting carrots. The cake was not the growing kind, but the most delicious kind: Carrot. She would have eaten half the cake, but Cheshire already had.

"You weren't even exercising, just sitting—drawing!" She stormed, a tempest in a tea cup as she leaned over the table, trying to steal his most recent piece of cake.

"It's called a drawing *exercise*," he said, holding his food over and behind his head.

Huffing, Lam fell back into her seat. "That doesn't count."

"Why not?" He pointed with his fork, gilded with frosting, and speared though an oversized piece of cake. "I don't need to do physical exercises as much so I did brain exercises. Really, I should be praised for stepping out of my comfort zone."

Before he could finish, Lam's primal instincts took over. Her mouth closed around his fork, and the sweet, buttery taste of cake was all she noticed for all of half a second. Then her eyes opened and met Cheshire's—orange eyes shifted to yellow to red while his mouth hung open.

Lam fell back in her chair and looked up at Hare. "Is there any more food?" It was incredible, she couldn't yet feel the itchy heat of embarrassment creeping up her neck.

Hare looked over at her, eyebrows raised. "If you're really that hungry, you can go gather your own food." A smile pulled his face as he nodded to the thunderstruck Cheshire. "Cheshire can go with you, I think there's more edible stuff farther into the woods."

Rudyard, inhaling water, started to gesticulate wildly. "What are you—" Cough, "The fact—" He waved his arms, pointing from Hare to Cheshire to Lam to Hare. "Un—" Cough, "accept—"

Mack started patting Rudyard on the back. Eyes turning to Lam, Mack nodded towards the door. Blushing, Lam did as she was told.

~

SHE WANTED to think she could outrun Cheshire, but seeing as she couldn't even do that in her imagination, it was never going to happen.

"Did it taste better?"

Her nose wrinkled involuntarily. "No."

Hands came in and out of sight with every swing of his arms. "That's funny, because you seemed to enjoy it more."

Crouching down, she poked at one of the non-poisonous fruits. "I was hungry."

Floating to block her view, he stared up and smiled, hiding the fruit and also closing her windpipe. He was close, very close. His eyes were bright and pointed teeth shone in a smile.

'I see you have made a new friend, the boy with the teal hair. I hope he doesn't worm his way into your heart.'

Lam ran one of her hands over the soft, warm skin of his face as she had when he'd come the night before.

'Are you here to watch me cry?'

'I'm here for you.'

As her fingers grazed his lips, a slight shiver ran through his body.

'Intently, I mean. I have to watch anyone and everyone around you.'

'What about me?'

Her head fell towards his as lips parted in surprise. Gently, their foreheads bumped one another.

'You might not want to kiss someone right in front of me.'

She had never seen his eyes so close up. Now she could see they glowed in the shadow cast by her, and the colors danced like curtains on the breeze.

'Well, my dear, then you have every romantic fool and half the boys in Wonderland.'

Lam smiled down at his wide eyes and his complete bafflement, tracing the lines of his surprise with her fingers. Now her face was the one pulled into a impish smile.

"Now." She patted his cheek. "How does it feel to be the fool?" Sitting back up, she grabbed a fruit that rested next to her. Her teeth dug into the soft flesh of the fruit as she stood and walked away.

It was a long time before Cheshire got up.

CHAPTER

TWENTY-ONE

L am's feet moved smoothly over the uneven floor to her room. Her hand twisted the brass handle as she pushed inside. The room itself was rather normal, except that it was filled with odd things, vaguely organized by century.

Her eyes were on the dresser as her mind ran over the drills she had learned that day. For the most part, Hare was teaching her defensive plays, but they had started to do more offensive moves, and he said they would do even more tomorrow. Her body was caught between excitement and exhaustion, leaving her thoughts to wander over the practice field.

After changing and drinking the last three drops of the gold potion, Lam slid into the bed, her body finally getting to rest. Her mind on the other hand...

THE DARK CAME into focus in waves of blue-green light. It took several moments for Lam to register that what she was looking at was water. Trapped behind thick glass, it rippled and twisted the distant light from above. Her hand reached forward to press it, but it wasn't glass at all. Fingers sank into freezing water, breaking the layer of ice. For some reason, the water didn't spill though. Lam's arm submerged deeper—wrist, elbow, and finally shoulder. The further she stretched in, the warmer the water got.

Suddenly the world around her—the tunnel—contracted. Her feet sank into the cracking ice, and her head snapped to watch as a thick wind was blown through the path. Rushing filled her ears, and fear hid in her heart. A flood of something was rolling though the pipe, invisible to her, but there all the same. As if it was letting out a sigh, the tunnel relaxed. Curiosity led her down the direction that the wind was going. Gradually, the path itself turned, curving so Lam was now walking perpendicular to the pull of gravity. Her hair fell into her view and was pushed aside so she could look down the passages that shot off from the hall she was on. With every step, her feet sank slightly into the water, but never deeply, as if it was holding her to the path.

Lam's movements sped faster and faster, till she was running down the hall. It was...magical, unique in a way she couldn't even begin to understand. Her right hand trailed in the water as she raced. There, just ahead, sat a door. By now, Lam was used to running straight down, but the thought of entering a space that might not have the same magic gravity filled her with trepidation. Slowly, she reached for the handles of the fluid double doors. In a rush of wind, Lam and the doors were pushed forward.

Her body flipped as it fell, sending her end over end. Gasping, Lam caught sight of the room around her, though to call it a room would be a painful understatement. It stretched wide and vast, filled with balconies and twisting staircases. Lam crashed through the floor with a fountain of dislodged water. Icy liquid caught her, seeped into her, clutching at her, calling her to stay. It thrummed around her, cold giving way to warm, giving way to hot. The tension in her body fell away, carried by the slow beat.

Ba-dum.

It was a weight more than a sound, a pressure that was getting heavier and louder.

"Lam?!" The word was distant, unimportant in the warm bliss that surrounded her. "Lam!" So frantic. So afraid. He was always scared for her safety...

In the water, Lam's eyes shot open at the same moment Cheshire grabbed her arm. Through the cold and past the ice, he pulled her, till they both collapsed on the thick floor.

"What are you doing here?"

Lam flipped her hair back, over her neck and shoulders. "Dreaming. What are you doing here?"

"This is my—" He bit of the end of his statement and switched to, "Dream. You're in my dream."

Ba-dum.

Finally, her eyes snagged on him. His hair was plastered to one side of his face, even as his curls fought to reform. His lashes seemed darker, most likely from the water, and his eyes were a mix of purple and pink. For clothes, he wore a loose black shirt and black pants. He looked older—slightly so, not quite Old Cheshire's age.

"Well," Lam's eyes couldn't comfortably rest anywhere on him, "how in Wonderland did I get into your dream then?"

His eyes, too, were on the move. "I... Well." They were turning red, roving over the balconies behind Lam. "I guess I didn't keep you out."

Twisting her hair, Lam dislodged a small pool of water from it. "But how did I get in?"

"You wanted to, I guess."

"You're trying to tell me that people can get into anyone else's dreams merely by wanting to if the other person simply doesn't keep them out?"

"No, there has to be a connection." The red had bled onto his face, leaving the eyes he turned to Lam filling with pinks and purples.

A pensive, swirling feeling rested in her gut. "What kind of connection?"

"It could be anything that Wonderland recognizes." His voice was a mutter and the red had subsided, turning into dark green in his eyes. "It could be my mission to protect you, which I swore on my joker status to fulfill. It could be that we both drank the potion from Hare." Cheshire looked away again. "...It could be a lot of things."

Already Lam had grown slightly bored by his logical ramblings and was looking around the room in wonder. "This is your dream? It's...gorgeous." The steps dripped down like twisting waterfalls, while the balconies they reached were packed with artifacts, books, and weapons. "It's—" Leaping to her feet Lam, stared down at the sopping boy. "It's your heart!"

"What?"

"It is, isn't it!" Lam was grinning, her feet ready to explore. "This is your heart!"

"You don't know—"

"Oh yes I do!" Spinning on her heel, Lam ran to the nearest staircase and ran up the fall. The liquid railing was filled with floating vines that burst from the water with cyan blooms. Everywhere Lam looked, she found something else beautiful and strange. She had never thought a heart could hold so much light, or movement, or ice. Her feet skipped onto the first balcony and she watched the moving paintings that hung on the wall, artworks of sunny days in the forest and training with Hare, pantings of unbirthdays and reading to Shire. With a sharp jump of her own heart, Lam's eyes fell on the largest painting.

The portrait stood at ten feet tall and was wider than her wingspan. In it sat a girl, her bright red hair falling over her shoulders in heart shaped curls, her hands holding a tiny wall of cards she used to defend herself. Annoyance and a shocked kind of joy were held in her eyes as a disembodied hand grabbed three of the cards. The dark markings of her face were sharp against the rosy paleness of her skin and every one of her freckles was held in exquisite detail.

It was stunning...and it was her.

The moment had seemed so insignificant to her. Just another card game. Just another time the joker had shown his prowess. But nothing about this artwork was *just*. Every line, every inch was lovingly documented, rendered to shine even more real then the initial moment. Lam could find as many words as she might like to describe it, but nothing would suffice.

"I swear not every part of my heart is like this." His words were soft and self deprecating, as if the painting was a silly mistake he forgot to take down.

Water met water as Lam's tears fell, and she turned to him. "You did this?"

Surprise was twisting every inch of him, drawing his hand to cup the back of his neck and his other to tap his leg. "Well, my subconscious did."

"And you have more?"

"I—" And they both stood in silence. He had rendered her in gorgeous clarity, and she wanted more. The ground they were finding to stand on felt like clouds, fanciful and insubstantial—like a wish, like a dream. And Lam could never remember how it ended.

TWENTY-TWO

No more dreams visited Lam that night, or at least none she remembered. The room seemed shockingly cold, and, for a long time, Lam stayed curled up in the bed. Her eyes eventually forced their way open. Lam sat up and looked around the room. The same odd assortment of objects greeted her, and her gaze soon slipped to the dresser.

Even as she walked over to grab her clothes, Lam couldn't shake the strangely sweet feeling of her dream. Was it real? Had Cheshire shared a dream with her? Had it all been in her head? Questions came and organized themselves as she took off her nightdress and pulled on a pair of pants and a dark brown shirt. Her spiraling thoughts continued as she stepped from her room and closed the door.

It seemed Rudyard, too, had also just woken up, still blinking the night away. Nodding to him, she entered the bright kitchen lined with wood shelves and no cabinets. She was surprised to see Old Cheshire and Shire sitting at the table now laden with flap-jacks. Old Cheshire gave Lam a tired nod as he tried to keep both Cheshires off of the syrup.

At this point, Cheshire went invisible and tried to get past him that way, but Old Cheshire cocked his head and shot out his arm just in time to stop Cheshire.

"You will have to teach me that," Lam said, sliding on to the bench next to Cheshire.

"Well, when you've raised as many invisible people as me," he shrugged, "it's almost as easy as seeing."

Lam stabbed a stack of flap-jacks with one of the forks on the table and used a clean plate. Over them, she poured syrup.

"Why does she get to have more than me?" Cheshire became visible and tried to trade plates with Lam, his hand avoiding hers.

"Because," Old Cheshire stopped him with a glare, "that's your second plate and the first one was more syrup than flap-jacks."

Huffing and sitting back, Cheshire's eyes turned everywhere but on Lam.

"Cheshire, look what I can do!" Shire said, wiggling from Old Cheshire's arm and jumping down from his seat. He closed his eyes and for a moment he became slightly see-through.

Sweeping him up, Cheshire started to tickle him. "You should have shown me that earlier!"

Shire was laughing too much to say anything.

Rudyard sat in the wonky chair Lam had used the evening before and it took a moment before he could really focus on the food. "Did you eat all of the flap-jacks?"

"Don't worry, more are on the way," Mack called from the stove. He and Hatter manned baking, wearing matching aprons.

Hatter turned around with a flourish. "Flap-jacks are served, my knave."

Rudyard made a face, "Don't call me a knave." But he didn't protest when Hatter laid a thick stack on his plate.

"To me," Hatter said, laying the pan back on the stove, "you will always be the knave that put Brussels sprouts in my morning tea."

Cheshire gave Rudyard an appraising look and nodded.

Old Cheshire sighed. "Hatter, you have sentenced me to Brussels sprouts in my tea."

Just then, Hare came out from his room, his fur sticking up around his ears, the gold in his eye thicker than usual. Both of his eyes blinked out of sync as he stared at Lam. "Lam, are you still not done eating?"

Lam threw up her hands, lifting the fork, then stabbed through her first bite. "You just got out of bed."

He blinked dazedly and she wondered if any dreams came out of his gold eye.

"My gold eye melts all the dreams I make."

"Why is it that all of you can read my mind?" Her voice was muffled around her square of syrupy pancake.

Cheshire, Old Cheshire, Hare, and even Mack shook their heads.

"It's more like we're really good guessers," Cheshire said through a mouthful of syrup.

Wrinkles were pressed into her nose. "Well, could you please stop guessing. My face already gives away more than it should."

Cheshire smirked, finally giving her his full attention. "I'd say your mouth says more." His eyes completed the transformation into the expression of the night before.

Handing Mack the spatula and wiping his hands, Hatter gestured to his room. "Lam, will you come with me?"

Lam let out a slow breath though her nose, trying to stop the blush invading her cheeks. Her eyes flicked to Cheshire, who's pink and green eyes were firmly staring at Hatter, before following the advisor.

"All right…" Dramatically stepping into his room, Hatter walked over to a wall covered in rolls of fabric. Either he had brought half his work supplies here, or Hare was a great collector of fine fabrics. Both options seemed strangely likely. "I need to make your ball gown." He pulled out a sheer, dark blue fabric. "The theme is night sky, and I would love to know what you're looking for."

Stepping lightly, Lam ran her finger over a dark blue velvet. She loved that he always asked her opinion, always brought her ideas to reality just how she liked, even when she was picky. "Something with lots of layers…"

Hatter nodded at her customary request.

A smile tugged at her lips as she flared her hand on a shear silk. "And can you put some of the stars on the inner layers, so there's lots of depth?"

Hatter nodded again, pulling out his notepad and marking both the silk and velvet.

"Oh," she bounced up and down, "can I have tall velvet boots!"

Tapping his pen to his lips, he dragged his eyes over the fabrics. "I do have those old ones of the queen."

"Yes! Thank you!" Excitement was making her move faster.

As Lam went on about all the things Hatter could do, Hare appeared in the doorway.

"Oi, Queen, it's time to run though your paces."

Lam let her arms fall from her last addition of gold dust on her skin. Instantly, she felt foolish, standing there, asking for more riches in one gown than most people saw in a lifetime.

Hare smiled and raised his chin. "Maybe next time we'll have you practice in a ball gown."

Lam grinned, hugged Hatter, and ran back to her room to grab her axe.

$\sim$

Her axe swung at her side as she lifted her chin to stare up at Hare. They stood in the same clearing they had yesterday, and once again, Cheshire was climbing the oak to watch.

"What are we doing today?"

"Much of what we did yesterday." Pulling her axe up with his, Hare handed her a mess of leather. "Don't hold your axe like that. Strap it to your back with this."

Twisting it in her hands, Lam found that it was basically a wearable pouch for her axe: one large pocket attached to two long straps that went over her shoulders connected with one smaller strap in the front and one behind her neck. Lam pulled the strap over her head and found that it rested quite comfortably on her body, the bottom hovering right above her hips, low enough that her axe handle would not be sticking far over her head. They started by just learning how to take on and off her axe then how to lock the handle with the smaller strap at her neck.

An hour later, the blade of her axe silently sliced though the air where an imaginary opponent stood. Under and up the chest plate, then across the stomach, finally up again to cut off its arm and let it bleed on the ground.

"Left handed."

Lam took in the call and did the entire motion again but reversed, finally cutting off the opponents left hand.

"Right handed."

Confidence rose in her, getting faster with each time.

"Ambidextrous."

Freezing, Lam's axe head dropped towards the ground. She turned around to face Hare. "What? You didn't teach me that."

He nodded to something past her. "Then you're dead."

"When am I ever going to fight someone who's ambidextrous?" Embarrassment and annoyance colored her voice.

"You'd be surprised." Hare threw his axe from hand to hand. "Although most are born and raised with a dominate hand, many fighters learn to use both." He nodded to Cheshire, sitting in his tree. "And some are lucky enough to be born that way."

Lam's lips parted and she stared up at the watching joker. *Another advantage he was born with.* It seemed everything about Cheshire made him a more effective fighter—his powers, his habits, it could even be argued that his smaller size benefited his style. Or perhaps his style was just an amalgamation of the things that came easiest.

"You can stop staring now." Hare cleaned his claws with the tip of his axe.

Blushing, Lam turned and tried to manipulate the move to fit someone double wielding. Up, across, her axe was now on what would be their right side so she just pushed past and though both arms.

"Good, now what if their arms are down, or they move them out of the way?"

Lam's eyes sharpened, and she felt a familiar rush though her body. Up, across, her foot moved forward and she sliced what would be their shoulders.

"Excellent. Now there are three at once."

Her back foot swept out, knocking her fist opponent's legs as her axe cut the second's lower abdomen. She could almost see the intestines falling out of them. The other stumbled as she rose to take on the third. The butt of her axe caught them in the face and she flipped it to cut up their sternum.

Clapping sounded from behind her and she moved on instinct. Hare caught her swinging blade between his hands. "Slow, child." Studying her face he saw something he had wanted but not expected. "It seems…" His eye fell to her questioning ones and he shook his head. "Again. The third could have killed you if they were a fifth the warrior I am."

Lam flicked her blade to get non existent blood off of it before she stared at her hands. "How did I—"

"Back to work."

IT WAS two more hours before she was allowed a break. Rudyard looked like he was about to hit Hare.

"This is none of your business," Hare said, crossing his arms.

"Not my business?" Rudyard waved his hand as if slapping the air. "This is my sister."

Lam looked up from her water flask. "Rudyard," she rested her hand on his arm, "this isn't your war." Red eyes turned to rubies as they rose to her brother's. "Better to bite the bullet then be bitten by the snake."

Rudyard's mouth hung slack, even though he was the one to tell her those words. He just could never imagine her speaking of the Prince of White Chess if she didn't have to.

"Thank you." Hare spun his axe in a hypnotic motion. "Now, back to work. You're getting sloppy, Lam."

Lifting her chin and rolling out her shoulders, Lam set down the water and grabbed the axe from her back.

It was another four hours before she was done for the day. There had been breaks and lulls when Hare was demonstrating or explaining something, and she'd had several water breaks. When they were finally done, she walked over to Cheshire, a habit that she was quickly getting used to.

After a few silent moments, where only the fireflies spoke, Cheshire walked down the tree and sat beside her.

"You can't stay quiet for long."

He knelt beside her, his eyes watching the bugs as well. "Have I said anything?"

"In your own way."

Twisting, he leaned against the tree with her. A sigh was pushed out heavily. "I was silent for years outside your door."

Finally, her eyes drifted to him. She was back in the library. Her fifteen-year-old arms were too short to reach the book, even as she stood on the ladder. She knew she should have rolled it over but it had seemed like too much work from the ground. As though through magic, the book wormed it's way out of the shelf and fell. Fear that the ancient book would hit the tile floor far below made Lam lean even farther out. Gravity finally got its hands around her and she began to tip. Both she and the book would fall and there was nothing left for her to do.

A pressure—not of air, or gravity, or even fate—grabbed her shoulder and halted the book's path. Air was pushed onto her cheek, but it was warm and sweet, so different from the chilly room. The ghost didn't say a word as it handed her the book and she had only just thanked it as she ran to tell her mother the house was haunted.

Finally, she could see him.

"Do you have a bias against talking?"

"No." His surprise didn't hide the purple tracing the edge of his iris. "Why would you think that?"

Her gaze cut away from him and to the flower she was

spinning in her hands. "You just seem to avoid telling me anything."

"I've told you things. Or...at least as much as I can."

"I wonder..." Her body fell towards his, her shoulder, the same shoulder he'd pushed so long ago, now hitting his.

Neither of them could keep the red from their eyes, but Lam's was permanent and his was bleeding. "You wonder what, Princess?"

"How many paintings you've made of me."

He twisted away, making a face. "Two, I'm sure."

"Two?" A sly grin slid onto her face and she batted her lashes. "I only remember one."

"The other is you drenched in sweat holding your battle axe incorrectly while Hare fixes your grip for the hundredth time. I will never be able to get the image from my eyelids and, in all likelihood, my heart."

FOR DINNER they had bangers and mash, which Cheshire would only eat doused in syrup.

Rudyard looked at Cheshire, appalled at his table manners. "I swear, you are going to single handedly bring the maple population to extinction."

Then Hare kicked his dirt-caked shoes on to the table and Rudyard grimaced.

"So what's the plan?" Hare picked at his teeth with a small bone. "Are you all leaving tomorrow or the day after."

"Tomorrow." Hatter cut a sausage with precision. "The ball is tomorrow night, and the last game is the day after."

Hare looked up in what Lam took to be thought until she noted the calendar pasted to the ceiling. "So it is." The Joker catapulted his fork into the eighteenth day of the silk moon, matching how he'd crossed off the last seventeen.

Rudyard, trying to ignore the odd spectacle, leaned forward. "Should we leave tonight?"

Cheshire was the one to shake his head. "The whole reason you're here is so no one will try to kill you. If the people after you are half as dedicated as they seem, they'll have assassins up and down the road to Hearts." He shrugged as he ran his tongue over his back teeth. "Plus, I don't really feel like watching out for two heads tonight."

The words fell heavy on Lam's shoulders, reminding her that she, too, needed to rest.

Noticing her fatigue, Hare took down his boots and leaned over the table. "Here, this will help with the soreness and bruising."

Lam studied the glass bottle with a pearlescent white liquid inside. The shaking legs she had been trying to ignore started to shake her entire body and she nodded, not able to speak. The weight of her head, her arms, and her shoulders all started to compound and she tilted forward before someone caught her. Voices spoke over her, trying to tell the world what should happen next, but it was all too far beyond Lam. Perhaps she should have tried harder to listen. Perhaps it was important. Perhaps her ignorance made her a fool.

There are always a lot of things that can be true, but the only thing that was true to Lam in that moment was the comfort of strong arms lifting her. It reminded her of stories, the young joker carrying the half-sleeping princess to some-where safe, or at least quiet. He didn't speak as he turned the handle and pushed the door open to her room, so she was forced to break the silence with tired lips and slurred words, "Thank you."

"It's my..."

She braced for him to say *job.*

"...pleasure."

Her tension released and a smile grew on her mouth as he laid her on the bed and pulled back the covers. "You're always so gentle with me..." Her heavy hand blindly lifted to find one of his. "You act as if you'll break me if you touch me for too long."

He folded the sheets over her, and his other hand brushed her cheek. "I'm not scared of breaking you." The silence finished his statement and, once it had, he stood.

"Sleep well, Lam."

Somewhere, between pauses and touches, they had both forgotten the empty bottle on her bedside. Somehow, in the moments they stole, they forgot how easy it is to be caught in a nightmare.

But someone would remind them.

TWENTY-THREE

The dream came into focus slower than usual, wisps of mist becoming a small, broken-down home. It was no larger than a guard tower, with a circular room off center at the top. She had no idea why she was there, but found it impossible not to walk towards the home. As she got closer, misty shapes appeared. Children walking, children feeding chickens, but most often children walking to and from a mining shaft. The sight was strange, like a silent play.

She walked to the front door, but felt as if she should find another way in. She found a ladder behind some hay bales and used it to get as high as she could. If she stretched, she could just reach the lowest part of the roof... With much scrambling, she managed to get to the top of the roof and could look in through the stained glass windows into the highest room.

On the bed sat a boy hidden by shadows. Before him, misty images formed, similar to the ones in the yard but these were always the same two children: A boy, small and skinny, and a girl with long black hair and the most beautiful face

Lam had ever seen. Silent vignettes filled the room—the girl teaching the boy to spin, the girl teaching the boy to sew, the girl teaching the boy to draw. But the one that kept playing over and over again, in the center of the room, was the girl teaching the boy to dance. The boy flushed, unable to look the girl in the eye.

The boy on the bed gave a soft, heartbroken sound as he started to cry. Leaving his head bowed, he took the place of the fantom boy. All the other mist figures disappeared as they danced around the room. The girl laughed but with no sound, like one of the silent movies Lam had gone to see. Then she, too, disappeared into mist. He was still crying, letting the tears hit the stone floor. His feet carried him to the far wall and a gasp was strangled in Lam's mouth. Masks. Hundreds upon hundreds of masks. All different expressions and materials, but none a true smile. He took one with a calm, slightly disturbing expression.

"Do you know what death looks like?"

Lam whipped around. It was the Storyteller—the boy—sitting inches away. The mask bore its blank eyes into her skin, taking in her shock and horror.

"Well, now. You look like you've see a ghost." The Story-teller leaned in until his mask was all she could see. "So, Princess, how does my past make you feel?"

"Alone." Her voice held the edge of broken clay.

He tilted his head. "Good." Ice coated his tongue and bled into his words. "At least you have that small similarity to me."

"Who was she?" She couldn't stop the words and he couldn't stop the rage that lifted his shoulders.

"Don't worry." He grabbed her head in one gloved hand, fingers digging though her hair to break her skull. "You're never going to meet her."

~

SHAKING, Lam opened her eyes. She hadn't had nightmares often, but she'd always had an active imagination. She would find swords in shadows, monsters in the molding, and blood on the floor boards. Her fears were dancing around her like painted stars, but it would get better if she stood.

Getting out of bed was its own from of practice. Slowly, she put on a simple, red dress, not all that different from the nightgown she took off. When she came out, all the food had already been eaten. She looked mournfully at the few crumbs on Rudyard's plate.

"Your food is in the forest," Hare said from where he cleaned his axe.

"Now, really," Rudyard started, but Lam had already gone upstairs. She kept telling herself that she really did want this, but, currently, that was hard to believe.

Cheshire was there, hanging upside down from a tree branch. When he spotted her, he flipped down and walked over to meet her.

"Good morning." Then he looked up into the sky. "Or is it, good afternoon? Anyway, are you ready?"

Lam looked up, still a little groggy. "For what?"

"The ball." He took in her bleary eyes and the pillow marks on her face. "Really, I don't understand why you people have so many of them."

"It's a great way to meet your equals and socialize with other nobles," she recited, saying the words with the exact same inflections that her mother would always use. Lam always liked to go to balls—everyone dressed up, dancing and eating. How could she not love them? "What is there to be ready for?"

Humming, Cheshire watched her pick some edible flowers. "It will be the last time to talk to the other contestants before you go into hand to hand combat with them."

"It's too bad that there are no chess cards. That way I could know for sure if I could beat them." Lam caught his grin as she turned around.

"But there is no card for you," he countered as they both sat.

"I guess you're right." She bit into the spicy orange flower. "Until I become a joker, that is."

Cheshire leaned back, braced by his arms. "You know, most games with cards don't include the jokers."

"I guess you're right," she shrugged. "Most of the time we would just use the jokers as replacements for any cards we lost."

Cheshire grimaced. "You drew over me."

Her laugh was a little dry and shot pain to her core. "It's not you, just like the king of hearts isn't my father."

Cheshire stole one of Lam's flowers and she didn't even bother to try and get it back.

"If you were a card, what card do you think you would be?"

"Hmm..." Her fingers trailed in the grass, still slightly damp with dew. "Well, I'm a better fighter than Rudyard, but I don't hold as much influence as my father so...queen?"

Cheshire nodded and popped the flower into his mouth. This surprised Lam. The flower didn't taste sweet

His eyes rose to hers. "Tastes like home." As always, answering a question she never asked.

THE RIDE back to the Castle was blissfully uneventful. Lam slept most of the time—after drinking some of the fresh

batch of potion from Hare—and dreamed of a queen that brought clouds to cover the sky in mourning. She was pulled from her sleep when they entered Pulse.

"Well, its good to see someone's looking forward to the last game," Rudyard observed.

Curiosity and the sound of cheers coaxed Lam to look out the window. Flags, flowers, and the finery of the people of Hearts curved her lips into a smile. The songs of Hearts were overlayed with people calling for Princess Lam to take the Games' Crown. It was silly and beautiful and bleeding hearts grew in every window they passed.

"Congratulations, Lam." Cheshire's velvet voice was quiet and soft as he, too, stared out her window. "You've already won your people's hearts."

Her cheeks brightened and she stared at him from the corner of her eyes. "And what about your heart, Cheshire?"

"Oh." The seriousness of his tone disappeared. "You won that a long time ago."

Snorting, Lam looked back at the red and gold flags lining the sky. Out of every kingdom Lam had been to, her own was her favorite. Puppeteers danced their characters with children's tin solders while bakers linked arms with florists. Being the country with the most bountiful fields, even the poorest had plenty to eat and clothes covering their back. Under the guidance of her father and the switch to rotational farming, the soil—and thus their produce—had gotten even better.

Hands pressed to the glass, she watched people wave and toss her bleeding heart flowers. Her namesake was her favorite flower, with its delicate red or pink petals and wide, green leaves. Desperately, she wished her hands could reach though the clear wall and grab them before they fell to the ground. All too soon, the carriage was rolling to a stop outside the castle and Hatter was ushering her up the stairs.

"I have to see the dress on you."

She craned her neck back. "You already finished it?"

"Well, I have to see it on you to know if I'm really done, but it's all there."

"How? You asked me yesterday!"

He reached past her and turned the door nob. "I was on a bit of a time crunch, but I also assumed that you were going to ask for most of the things you did, so I already had all the embroidery done." Setting her to one side, he turned back to the two guards carrying the box that contained her dress. "It might be a little heavy, but nothing more than you're used to."

After the box was on the ground and the guards out the door, Hatter lifted the lid and pulled out his newest masterpiece.

Gasping, Lam stepped forward, consumed by its glory. The skirt was so full she estimated it was three feet across without any petticoats and with gold stars on every layer.- Grinning like a fool, Lam stepped up onto a dressing stool. After her old clothes were removed and the base layers donned, Hatter tied the skirt and bodice. Lam couldn't help lifting up one arm and letting the multilayered, sheer, bell sleeve drape. In this room, the night sky had come down, and it was her.

"It's..." she squeezed her eyes closed just feeling the dress.

"Perfect?" Hatter prompted. "Well, there's more."

Lam opened her eyes, before her stood knee heigh boots, freshly cleaned, the wood soles shinning.

"You need to stop this." She tilted her face up. "Hatter your work is perfect, perfect, perfect, perfect. Now, I'm not going to say it again." She crossed her arms and glared up at him in pure joy.

Quickly, Hatter tied her hair into tight plats pressed to her head and dusted her lids and cheeks with blues, purples, and a sparing spray of gold. Then he drew on the stars in gold, violet, red, yellow. When she turned to the mirror, she almost didn't recognize herself. She looked older. She looked more like a queen. She straightened and turned to Hatter.

"Now, just for the crown." He went to the corner and pulled out a golden masterpiece. Stars appeared to float, only held by invisible rods. "What do you think?" His eyes twinkled.

Lam pouted out her lower lip. "Quite ordinary. Really, I don't know why we keep you around."

He gave a little bow, hiding his smile. "Happy to serve."

As he finished, Rudyard and Cheshire came in, dressed for the occasion. Rudyard wore a black velvet vest embroidered with stars, over an elegantly simple shirt and dark blue pants, a dinner jacket draped over one arm. Cheshire was dressed similarly, though his vest was more of a midnight blue and had a one-shoulder cape on top.

"Are you ready?" Cheshire was giving her an appraising look. "Will you be able to dance in that?"

Lifting her skirts to alleviate some of the drag, she stepped from the stool and gave one of her practiced smiles. "Yes and yes."

"Actually—" Hatter turned her head to him with one bent finger. Over her lips, he painted in dark blue the shape of a heart. "Now you're ready."

Lam couldn't help glancing to Cheshire for his reaction. His eyes were firmly on the watch at his wrist, even if they were red. Not missing a beat, Rudyard led the way down the stairs, followed by Lam. Cheshire followed behind, his shoes pausing to avoid stepping on her dress. She could feel her bare neck, his eyes resting on it, and how it was now turning red.

"You look stunning." His voice was soft and honest again.

Lam looked back and up at him as they spiraled down the stairs. "You look great, too." Her eyes traced his face and the color of his eyes—a blue, quick to dance though other colors.

Glancing away, he laughed. "Well, the night sky matches my hair a little more."

"Never heard of a blood moon?" She swung her head to show off the hair.

"Nope." His smile grew, and he stepped down faster to stand next to her. "Only a love moon. That's what they're called in the Forest."

"Hmm, a very different picture... I like it."

They separated, and Lam and Rudyard rode with their parents, while Cheshire rode with Hatter in his carriage. It was wonderful to see the sun paint the clouds in shades of pink and purple. They made it just before the first stars came out. Lam would have stayed on the front steps all night; the soft music that trickled from the ball was all she needed. All too soon, another carriage was pulling up, and she was forced to go inside. Once again, she was amazed at the hall made for this one occasion. With towering pillars and an open roof, this one was even more breathtaking than the last. But this time, she did not stop or shake. She was the night, a force as unbreakable as the constellations.

As she glided down the stairs, arm linked with Rudyard's, she could tell that Hatter had outdone himself. She felt the gaze of hundreds of people.

"It's good to see you've gotten your strength back."

Lam could hear the approving smile in his voice.

She was glad she had him. "Just because I slept all the

way from the Forest doesn't mean I'm too exhausted to walk down some stairs."

"Not that kind of strength."

This time, when he let go and moved into the crowd, she did not seek sanctuary at the food, but clarity in a glimpse of the sea. As soon as she stepped out though the pillars, sea mist covered her. It felt wonderful, clinging to her skin. Her feet carried her far, till Lam stood inches away from the shear drop to the jagged rocks below. The crashing waves brought icy foam to the cliff, trying to grab her, to take her in. Its roar filled her ears and chest, somehow calming in its frantic power. Her misty breath joined its rolling fog, so insignificant, but still distinctly hers.

"Hello, My Fool."

Ice, deeper and more clawing than the mist, climbed up her back at the words, and she turned to see a nightmare painted to look like a star.

The Prince of White Chess wore an eight pointed star over his face, and the sleeves of his suit were made of gossamer, revealing the toned form of his arms. The entirety of his outline shown from the light steaming out of ball, now indistinct through fog.

"Why are you here?" The words where as sharp and heavy as a swing from her axe.

He stepped to the edge of the sea cliff, the metal tips of his boots resting on air. "Enjoying some fresh air." The side of his mask felt like it was burying itself in her throat.

"You didn't answer my question."

He turned to face her again. "Good! You have some semblance of intelligence." Clasping his arms behind his back, he shifted to face the ball. "Too bad it took you so long." Pulling something from his pocket, he stepped past her and pressed it into her hands. "Seven crowns on Teon tomorrow."

A mix of stomach acid and fear had climbed its way into her throat as hatred danced on her skin. The Prince of White Chess, Zacharie K. Queenside, was the one person that Lam truly hated. And the only person that could make her cry by doing something as simple as that.

Her eyes titled to the sky as her body shook. She couldn't cry. She wouldn't cry. She wasn't going to give him the satisfaction of seeing her cry. Anger tightened her fists and reminded her of what he had left her. In her hand, she held seven crowns—the highest form of currency—and a piece of shattered teacup, pulling blood from the finger that had clutched it. Zacharie was not known for his tact. He was known for winning. Something Lam too, was now known for. Lam threw out her hand and tossed all the gifts to the sea just as the horns blew.

ALL THE CONTESTANTS found their partners, Lam confidently striding to Teon. His outfit was one of the moon, and Lam could have sworn that he glowed.

Redness creeped into his face from his ears. "You look lovely, Lam."

"And you look blinding. How is it that you glow?"

He looked down as if noticing his apparel for the first time.

"Dyed with a rare mushroom found in the Forest," he shrugged, "That's about as much as I know."

Cheshire would know more. He would know exactly what type of mushroom it was and what all its side effects were. She grabbed Teon's hand, catching a glimpse of Cheshire dancing with a red pawn, his face smiling as the girl laughed. The music was soft and sweet, the type that carried you more than your partner did. Lam looked up at Teon, and he smiled, pulling her to the music. Lam couldn't help giggling as she spun around. She looked into Teon's face. His ears were redder than her hair.

"Lamprocapnos, there is something that I want to ask you. Or...tell you." Fear flashed in his eyes. "You don't have to say yes. But I would like to court you."

Lam felt her own face redden. This was a first. She didn't know what to say. She had thought that Teon might like her, but...

Her mouth moved before her mind, a formal reply kicking in, "I would love to discuss it with my parents."

Teon nodded, eyes scanning the people. "Yes, that's perfect. I'm sorry if this is sudden but things—" He cut himself off. His eyes locked back on her as his head tilted closer to hers. "Time itself is moving faster, it seems, and the sun on tomorrow's game is one I fear to meet."

When the music stopped, Teon bent down and kissed her hand. While his lips were still on her knuckles, he whispered, "Please remember, Princess, neither of us put our heads in this game. And think on my proposal."

Another hand grabbed the one at her side. As Teon raised his head, his eye caught on the boy now standing beside Lam. They all stood there for a moment, a beat, a shaky breath of air, in which Teon's face hardened and Lam watched the hand that had just held hers fall to his side.

Then, Cheshire was pulling her away and their feet rushed past dancers and chatters, her hand in his.

"Cheshire! You can't do that! I was talking to someone." Blood flushed her face as her heart raced in her chest. "It was very important!" Her whisper yell went ignored until they reached open ground.

Cheshire became visible, spinning around and letting go

of her hand. "You looked like you were about to scream for help."

"I did not!" Then Lam groaned and sank to a crouch.

It was all so confusing. She laid down, looking at the stars. She found Teon interesting, but the way he'd proposed courtship felt wildly off. Perhaps he loved her and had simply seen the prince talking to her and how terribly uncomfortable that made her. She groaned again, not sure what to feel.

Cheshire sat next to her. "Do you want to be courted?"

Lam turned her face to him. His arm was next to her head, lithe and strong.

"Not really? The idea was never important for me seeing as—" The memory of the prince was still to sharp to touch. "I just never thought there would ever be someone who would want to."

"Someone?" Cheshire's eyes were bright in the darkness, his hair whipped around by the wind.

Her heart caught on something in her chest.

He let his arm bend till he was leaning next to her. His eyes, colored red and gold, darting over her face. "Would it be weird if I courted you?"

Face to face, almost touching noses with him, their breath mixing in the misty air, her eyes stayed in his, waiting... But what was she waiting for? Did she love him? She thought of everything he did, everything he was, the way he would talk in his melodic voice, how he would look up to the sky in thought, how his eyes lit up when he saw sweets, his hand in hers. But there was something deeper, beyond anything he could do or say, something she was connected to. *Someone.*

Her eyes flicked to something distant, indistinct...or at least it should have been. White and white, the two young men Lam feared seeing the most, Teon's face was gaunt, ashen, empty like a statue that has been carved too much.

Beside him, the prince looked prideful, almost exultant as she stared. They were far, mist still crowded the space between her and them, but they weren't far enough. Hearts, why? Why did they have to see this?

Fear made her body arch from Cheshire's, but it was pain that made her stop—sharp, purple pain filling his eyes.

"Lam?" Her name seemed to cut his tongue as pink shown in his eyes. She could hurt him so easily, just by digging indifference into his chest.

Her eyes shuttered closed, and she was deep in a memory: *a tea cup—her tea cup—shattered on the ground all because she'd looked away when she should have guarded it.*

When she opened her eyes, she leaned closer, their noses next to one another, his head tilted. She saw his Adam's apple bob, his eyes matching her red. He waited.

Would it be weird if he courted her? Her tone was set when she spoke, though it was only whisper on his lips. "Yes."

Grinning, Cheshire pulled back. "Good, I find courting to be one of the stupidest things you humans have come up with." He switched to crouching, now facing her with his whole body. "You put rules on love." He found her real markings with his eyes, under the face paint. "We are just physically bound by it."

"How so?" She couldn't help looking to where Teon and Zacharie had stood, but they were gone from her sight.

"When we fall in love, we give away our heart. Humans don't have any ill effects from this." Her eyes shifted back to his in time to catch his eyebrows rise as a smile tried to break free of his teeth. "And that's solidly the saddest thing about you all."

Lam cupped his face and stared into his eyes. "Well, it's good to see you still have a heart."

Laughing, he pulled away, the light from the party too dim to show if his face was heated. "In a way, I guess."

Lam looked back at the party with tired eyes, wanting nothing more than to not go back. Again and again she stared at the spot were Teon and the prince had stood, hoping against hope that she'd imagined them.

"You know...it's still not to late to run away," he offered.

Lam shook her head, smiling as he laced his fingers through hers. "But we'd be running the wrong direction."

"Well then..." He rose, pulling her to her feet as well, "Will you run back with me?" His eyes danced red over a backdrop of purple and blue.

Her lips moved, but no air carried the silent 'back where?' from them.

His free hand found her ear and brushed a stray hair behind it. "To the dance." He smiled and his irises were consumed by red. "That is why we're here, isn't it?"

"That is one of the reasons." Her gaze fell from his and darted to the world behind him. "I also have to be here."

He pulled her even as he let go, leading her to the dance floor. "I would love it if I was also one of your reasons." He was such a fascinating mix of embarrassment and brazenness, of lines and curves.

The ambient sound of gossip and polite threats filled Lam's ears, but for some reason it was completely foreign. It should have been familiar, recognizable, comforting, but the person walking in front of her was all those things and so much more.

As they found their place on the floor, Lam couldn't help but stare at everything else. Gently, Cheshire spread his hand across the space beneath her left shoulder blade. It was warm and solid, and she could feel it far too much though her dress. Lifting his left hand, he let her make the next move. Slowly, she placed her left hand on his shoulder and her right in his hand. Something about the world had tunneled, and suddenly nothing else mattered.

"You look scared." His voice was loud and a whisper all at once, or perhaps she had made it deafening in her mind.

"I am." She wouldn't look at him till after. "I'm scared that you will step on my lovely shoes." There, now she could look.

"Have I ever given you reason to doubt my abilities?"

The music flowed into form, and Cheshire began to pull her towards himself. His thumb stroked her side as he pulled her closer, moved faster. People started shifting, Lam caught the eyes of another dancer and saw pure bafflement.

"Cheshire." Heat climbed its way up her face. "You have to slow down."

"Why?" What a stupidly brilliant question. Her boots clicked on the stone as he spun her in his arms. "Why are you chasing approval you don't care about?"

The question lodged in Lam's chest and she kept her eyes locked on his. "Because...I'm...supposed to."

The words fell flat between them and his eyes shifted through reds and pinks to hide in purples. "You really are a princess."

Lam shifted her hand from his shoulder to the back of his neck. "Is that a problem?"

A smile pulled his lips and a sigh pushed them open. "It's not a problem..." His hand fell from hers as he lifted her and spun. "But it is something. You live in a cage called a crown that even I can't get you out of."

"So I'm stuck here?"

Pulling away, he took all of her in. "Very few would think of your position as something to be stuck in..."

Laughter fell from her lips, but her fingers held tighter to his hand. Letting go of his neck, Lam let him spin her under their arms.

When they came back, Cheshire finished, "but I am among the few."

Smiling, Lam stepped back and bowed as the music faded. "I appreciate that."

"Now, all that stands in your way is pride and fear." He leaned and kissed her hand. "Tell me Lam, which will you give up first?"

TWENTY-FOUR

I am now understood why the Storyteller wore a mask. It would be so much simpler to be able to appear any way you so chose, it was so tiring to make the faces yourself.

She talked little and tried to not listen to the whispers. She got hundreds of compliments on her apparel from her hair to her boots, but behind them were gossip and questions the people had already decided to answer.

"I would say you look lovely, but I am not a fan of empty words." It was the fist time Lam had seen Elfin without her sister and the words were far from what she'd have expected.

"You think I don't look nice?"

The Princess of Red Chess turned her black eyes onto Lam, the bright red tips of her locks following like comets over the black night sky of her dress. "No. You look like a Storyteller...or a fairytale." Her lip curled the barest inch. "I just have no love for such things."

Before, Lam had thought Elfin a timid thing, but she had confused the silence of fear with the stillness of glowing coals. In many ways they were similar—Elfin was strangely short for a member of Chess, standing at the same hight as Lam, they both were sixteen, had older siblings, and both were set to inherit nothing.

"Well, I think you look lovely tonight."

Elfin's eyes flicked to Lam as tension shifted her expression. "Did your lover teach you that honesty."

"I don't have a lover." Lam's eyes felt pulled to search for Cheshire in the crowed.

A snort came from beside her. "Oh please, I'm not your father or mother. You can't honestly think I would believe that." Elfin played with the edge of one of her elbow length gloves. "And I see the way he looks at you." Her voice had fallen flat and hard.

Hair rose on Lam's arms, as her eyes stayed looking out over the party. "Do you fancy him?"

"So you admit it."

Turning her whole body to face her, Lam stared down the other Princess. "No, but I don't need to. You said you see the way *he* looks at me." Lam tilted her head, now searching the planes of Elfin's face. "Do you fancy Cheshire?"

Elfin's cheek reddened, but she kept her eyes on Lam. "No, because it's wrong to love someone from the other side."

Lam's face was pulled into a joyless grin. "I believe you just insulted both of our siblings." Lam stepped past Elfin, her eyes now locked on another princess. "And I do not take insults of my brother's character politely."

Lam moved past others—past liars and thieves, past the masks that Lam had taken for granted—till she came to a girl with her face shrouded by a starless night sky. The Princess of Spades was a black hole, from her gloved finger tips to her tightly curled hair, every visible piece of her was as dark as ink.

Lam tilted her head to her. "Ravine."

"Lam." Ravine, too, tilted her head. "I fear your night has not been as pleasant as you hoped."

Comfort from her voice released the tension in Lam's shoulders. "You could say that."

Ravine was two years older than Lam and had been the princess Lam enjoy being around the most. When they chatted, she would always make educated guesses, letting Lam fill in the details as she shared her worries. She wore a mask for much of her life, but it was a mask of glass—not concealing, but sometimes suffocating.

"It seems that no one can really relax the day before a friendly battle."

Ravine shifted, the glass beads on the edge of her veil clicking together. "Perhaps. But I fear it will not be as friendly as we might hope." Her gloved hands smoothed her skirts, shaking slightly. "I feel blood in the water."

Lam's skin pricked and her eyes were brought back to the dance floor. "Well then, let's hope its not ours."

Ravine made a humming sound. "But if not ours...then whose?"

Black boots made their way to stand next to Ravine, and Ravenel's eyes fell to Lam's. He, too, wore a black shroud, though his was shear and only covered his eyes. Over his body was a black coat, lined in deep blue fur and adorned with countless gold stars. Unlike his twin, Ravenel did not hide, but watched for the shadows cast by spotlights.

"Lamprocapnos." His head only entertained the idea of bowing.

"Ravenel." Curtsying, Lam made up for his lack. "How do you fare?"

"Cold." Only a prince of Spades, the coldest kingdom in Wonderland, would clam it was cold on a early spring night.

"And oppressed." His eyes rose to the open sky. "I hate when the stars are watching."

Lam, too, looked up. "Do they make you feel small?"

"Insignificant," he corrected.

Lam didn't catch whatever he handed his sister, the hand that had been in his pocket now hanging empty at his side, as his other tilted a glass of wine to his lips. "When I die fully, bury me ten feet under ground."

Ravine straightened next to him, and clenched what he had given her. "I will be sure to do so."

Ravenel shifted his gaze to his sister. He took on a expression that Rudyard sometimes wore—affection and fear, the knife edge that all siblings running into shadows will walk. "Thank you." The biting caution was turned on the rest of the room and his gaze snagged on a pair standing not too far away. "Keep an eye on those two." The words were low, but meant for Lam, not his sister. It was even stranger to think that he could care for her safety as well.

Following his gaze, Lam found the two remaining contestants in the final round. Their white clothes, matching yet distinct, clearly signaled their kingdom, but when Lam met the eyes of the male, he only nodded slightly and tipped his glass to his lips.

"Who are they?"

"Bishops, the informants and advisors to the King of White Chess." Ravenel didn't hide the sneer that twitched his nose. "That entire court is cursed."

"I fear it is cruel to speak of curses," his sister cautioned, lifting a glass from a passing tray. "They tend to bleed."

Sighing, he leaned towards her and kissed her on the cheek though the veil. "Fair enough. Though I fear that they also tend to hide."

Then he nodded to Lam. "May the King win."

"And may the Fool find his path." She finished. It was strange to think that this age-old saying had been taught to both of them by different teachers at different times, and yet connected them.

~

WHEN THE FINAL DANCE CAME, Teon seemed nowhere to be found. Lam itched all over as she stared at the dance floor. In the end, she stood on the sidelines the entire time, watching others move across the floor and searching the crowd for the person she was supposed to join.

Goodbyes seemed to drag on and on. Compliments that seemed ever more bitter and bland filled Lam's ears and weighed her down. Eventually, they had made it to the carriage and she could finally sit down. The ride seemed shorter than before and Lam was grateful. She honestly didn't think she could keep her eyes open any longer.

That night she was far too tired to brush her teeth, too tired to change into bed clothes...too tired to take Hare's potion.

~

HER DREAM BROUGHT her to a large home—a castle if she wasn't mistaken. She let her hand trail along the black wall-paper of ravens and rose petals. The hall was large and elegant, the walls covered in paintings. Three little girls kept appearing throughout the artwork: all of them drawing, the middle girl being drawn by the other two, the oldest reading to the younger while the middle looked over her shoulder, the youngest and oldest playing in the garden as the middle girl looking sadly on. Lam recognized the middle girl. How could she forget her long black hair, her pale skin, her big gray eyes? She turned away and continued. Like in most dreams, she knew exactly where to go, as if there was an invisible string between her and where she was supposed to be, a noose around her soul.

As Lam got closer to the hanging pole, she started to hear music. Entering a large room, she saw it held nothing but a piano. The windows covered in the ghosts of black shears and only a candle spilling onto the far keys to light the pianist—a girl, her fingers pouring out a sad and beautiful song that felt like rain. Her raven hair disappeared into the dark of the room while the snow white of her skin shown in the candlelight. Lam's eyes widened as her breath caught and a story that she'd never considered a tragedy sang though her mind.

Just then, a woman, also with long black hair and pale skin, came in through the only other door.

"Leyna, I've told you not to play." The queen stopped, hands on hips, glaring at the girl, who could only be her daughter. "Now run up to bed. Your sisters are already there."

The girl sagged. "Yes, mother." As she walked towards the door her mother shrank away, as if to not catch something her daughter had. When the girl walked out of the room, the scene started over again.

"Tragic, isn't it."

Fear caught in Lam's mouth and ran down her throat as she looked back over. He sat there on the piano, his boots pressing into the melted wax, staring down at the girl. When he turned from his love, Lam could see a crying mask covered the Storyteller's face. "Her own mother wouldn't touch her." Fingers dusted in black coal and palms covered in damaged fabric tightened their grip around the lip of the piano. The boy's anger was held in his back, in the cut of his shoulder against the pressing darkness.

"Why are you showing me this?"

Gently, he slid from the piano, shoes making no sound. "Because, I thought you might want to know the story of how I became a Storyteller." His words were frank and simple, but shook Lam to her core. Became. He had become a Storyteller. One of the seven god-like beings that led the living though the world. Had he, too, been led once?

Clasping his hands behind his back the same way Cheshire did, he began. "Once upon a time, long, long, long ago, there lived a boy..." A shadowy character danced along the walls as his story was told again. "...a small, kind, stupid, runt of a boy." The Storyteller's tone darkened with each word, and the shadow boy stumbled. "And when he was very young, he was sold." Another shadow, even darker on the wall wrapped around the boys neck and halted him. "To be a slave of the king." The shadow was brought to his knees, the awful play familiar but impossible for the shaking Lam to place. "He was sent far off, away from his siblings, away from his mother, away from even the king himself." The shadow king raised his hand, pointing to the door and in a flicker of wind the candle moved to show a different scene. "The boy was sent to mine in the dark." The pickaxe fell over and over, breaking the darkness around the boy. "But...the boy was not alone." Other children stepped out of the darkness and began to carve out the darkness with their picks. "So the boy gained a new family, a new home, and, soon, even a new ruler."

The candle flickered again and the music swelled, something sweet and fragile. "One day, a princess was sent to be the new slave master." A shadow with long, flowing hair was pulled, kicking from a carriage. "This was because her mother was jealous and could no longer stand to see her." One of the slave children held up a flower to the girl and she took it slowly. When her fingers touched it, blackness spread out and consumed the scene, blackness shifting into a view of the girl, who sat with a book on her lap. "The princess was very smart and kind, so she taught the slaves and didn't work them quite so hard." Setting down her book, the shadow girl took the hand the shadow boy offered her. "The boy fell in love with the girl, but..." Once again, where the girl's hand touched became black, spreading out like a plague. "...it was not meant to last."

A cold silence filled the room, the candles' light diminished by the story as it waited for the next line. The Storyteller himself straightened as if to keep from saying more. "The girl was killed, and the boy was forced to wander alone." The shadow boy came back, though he was older and shaking, his body weak as he collapsed in front of a staircase, spiraling into the sky. The masked boy stared at the ghost of his love. "That is all you need to know."

He turned to Lam, his mask starting to crack as the world around them disappeared to blackness.

"Sorry. I've never introduced myself." He bowed, his mask falling and cracking on the ground, but before Lam could see his face, her dream disappeared into wisps of mist. "My name is Tragedy."

LAM LOOKED at the very real room around her— red and pink wallpaper, desk, cards, rocking chair. But her mind was running over the dream—the girl, real stories, a past, and Tragedy.

Facts, memories, and what she was taught all tried to shuffle together, but it was like shuffling fortune-telling cards, playing cards, and rook cards together for a round of poker. The Storytellers were god-like beings said to control and record fate. They were supposed to have come around when Wonderland first made people, long before any hierarchies or kingdoms had formed. It was said that the twins—Romance and Comedy—formed Chess, while the sisters—Revenge, Mystery, and Fables—had made Cards. Adventure was said to have made the Forest all by himself. And Tragedy...

A dagger of the familiar sadness and a new beat of fear shot through Lam. It was said that Tragedy had died before any of his siblings had made anything. So, how? How did he become a storyteller? How? And why?

Unsettled, Lam turned over and met the sight of 7:20 AM. She shot out of bed, eyes wide and heart beating fast. Unlike the other games, this one started in the morning, in all of one hour and forty minutes. She ran all the way up to Hatter's studio, bare feet skidding on the marble floors, mind tripping over what she learned.

Classically, he didn't look up from his work. "Your armor is in your dressing room."

Pushing aside the thick velvet with shaking hands, Lam entered the changing room. Before her, gold-plated armor gleamed. It had been a while since she had worn a full suit and it took several tries to strap the pieces of the ornate armor over her body. Chainmail hung all the way down her neck, spilling under her sweetheart chest plate and dagger sharp pauldrons. Over her hands, delicate gauntlets slipped, guarding her knuckles with ruby points and hiding the shaking. Lam had thought she was prepared, that she understood what was about to happen. But standing, staring at herself as she draped the chainmail-veiled crown over her, added a numbing weight to it all. She was about to fight. She was about to enter a battle field—a small one, yes, one with rules, but not one that promised she would leave.

'I feel blood in the water.'
'The girl was killed...'
'You must promise me you will be safe.'
'My name is Tragedy.'

Fates' gold strings pulled her so hard, Lam though she might break. In the mirror stood a princess, a warrior, a queen. Tilting her head up, Lam saw a flash of gold under her chainmail veil but when she looked more closely, her cheek was back to normal. A spray of freckles and hollow heart telling her where she came from. Who she was doing this for?

"Can—" Lam clenched her fist against the shake in her voice as she walked from the behind the curtain. "Can some one help me with the chausses and leg plates?" Distantly, Lam stared down at her red pants. "I... I forgot how to strap them on." The admission brought a flush to her face and tears pricking at her eyes. Hearts, she was stupid. She couldn't do this. Not now, not today. Everything that happened the day before swirled with the dream, showing how little she understood, how high the walls rose over her head. She was no queen. Even then, she was running away from being a princess. She didn't deserve to carry the marks on her face or the armor on her back.

"That's alright."

Two words, calm and smooth, letting her tears fall from her face. Lam's welling eyes rose to Mack, his eyes on her shoulders as he repositioned her pauldrons.

"You never could figure out how to do that." Gently, he took the padding from her hands and began to tie them on, muttering as he did. "I wish I could have run more tests. The model who practiced in it said to was wonderful, but I hope it fits you even better. She said there was some pinching around the waist, but her proportions were slightly different. Is it uncomfortable at all?

Silently, Lam shook her head, wiping away the last of her tears. Mack had been making armor as long as Lam had been wearing it, but he never let himself be satisfied with his work.

"Of course I wish I could have tested it on you, but you were so busy before the beginning of the games, and I didn't want to distract you. Then we were in the Forest, and I had completely forgotten to bring it." The left leg clicked into place, holding to her body perfectly. "Is that to tight? Are there any uncomfortable spots."

Bending her leg, Lam tested the range. It was wonderful, like everything Mack made, but he still found something to fix, shifting the knee plate slightly. "I did rush that. I knew I should have made it thinner at the back, but I was worried it might fall off." His mutters became murmurs as he moved to the other leg, and Lam felt tears well up again.

When she blinked, her eyes opened on a much younger Mack, fretting with his first gauntlet. 'There are just so many parts!' He tried to straighten the pinky, but it stubbornly stayed curled in on itself. Annoyance was turning his cheeks pink and his eyes watery. He had been working on that one gauntlet for the past three months and it was some of the most complicated work he'd even done.

A younger, and much shorter, Rudyard walked over. 'Maybe you didn't do anything wrong.' Taking the metal from Mack's hands, he inspected the finger, twisting and straightening the pinky.

'Yay!' Lam raised her hands that were still soft, unmarred and uncalloused by the training she had just started. 'Mack made a gauntlet!'

Sixteen-year-old Lam laughed as she blinked away the memory.

"What is it?"

"Just remembering the first gauntlet you made."

Rudyard stepped from the other changing room, pulling on his crown—a gold circlet, studded with up-side-down hearts. "The one I fixed?" His smile shown bright in the refection of his gold armor. The gold painted him like a king, honoring the nature of his stance, the way he stood before them. Lam had never known what she would grow to be, but Rudyard always had. He had studied harder, talked more eloquently, and ruled more kindly than anyone else she had met, even if he had only ruled himself.

The three of them stood together, painted in early sunlight and gold. It was a moment that looked so much like a thousand ones before, but felt so different that it made your whole body hurt. Sixteen years they had been like that—Lam and her two older, wiser, doting brothers.

Hatter coughed, and Lam caught sight of his hand brushing his cheek. "It's time to go," was all he said, standing and ushering them to the carriage where Cheshire sat waiting.

TWENTY-FIVE

Once again, Lam, Rudyard, Cheshire, and Mack were all in the back of Hatter's carriage, but this time they weren't talking. Lam felt a thick sense of foreboding in the pit of her stomach. They spent the time playing rummy—Mack's main way of comforting her—and trying to stay present. But there was so much to think about: The Game, her dream, Teon, Cheshire, the prince's bet, and the twins of Spades' words.

It was only a short drive to the arena, and Lam was sure she wasn't the only one who was a little shaky as she stepped out. The arena was large and imposing, made from black and red marble. Even from a distance, Lam could hear the low thrum of tens of thousands of people.

This was the only game open to all, and it was also a holiday. Therefore, at least a fourth of the host kingdom showed up, and the other kingdoms would also have many representatives. Dread began to suffocate her, filling her chest and mouth.

"This is the point where we must leave you." Hatter and Mack looked at them, Hatter catching Lam's eye. "But we will be in the stands, always ready to come to your assistance."

Mack stepped forward and hugged Lam, then Rudyard. "Be safe, you two." The soft, orangey scent of the young man pushed tears from her eyes.

Laughing, she strapped her axe to her back. "I will. You stay safe, too." Ice and fire, Lam's feelings of fear ran down her sternum.

'If not ours… then whose?'

Not Mack's. Lam hoped, as Mack and Hatter walked away, that no one's blood would stain today.

"It's ok," Rudyard said, laying a hand on her shoulder, "everything will be fine."

"Contestants," a stout man, dressed in coordinator uniform, bowed to them, "right this way."

Lam shivered as they went down into the tunnels. They were unreasonably cold for spring.

"You made it!" There was Myla, her eyes even wider with concern, neck tinged green from her recent healing. She wore silver armor in the shape of an owl, its wings wrapping around her back, mouth open.

"You look great," Lam and Myla said in unison. Whether from their scattered nerves or the fact that they were so unlikely to say the same thing, they started to giggle, stifling it with their hands.

Only then did Lam think about the fact that she might have to fight Myla, or Rudyard for that matter. This thought cut off her laughter, and she straightened and looked around. This was the Cards tunnel, so the members of Chess were on the opposite side of the arena. Everyone was tense, as if the cool air had solidified in their bodies. Before she could catch anyone's gaze, the horns blew, and the chills on Lam's skin shivered into her bones.

She was walking, leading the pack, as was standard for the highest scorer. Anticipation was thick in her body, wrapping around her arms like a snake. Silently, she measured the weight of her axe on her back, counted her steps, walked out into the sun. Cheers and yells crowded her head, and a new sensation twisted inside her. Pride pulled her shoulders back and opened her eyes. She was winning.

Her eyes rose to the royal box across the stadium. The Prince of White Chess stared down at her, body draped in gold silk, one shoulder hosting the lifeless head of a infant jabberwock. The young king's head bore a snake-like crown. This time, it wasn't his words that echoed in her head, but the cheers of thousands.

Turning, she caught Cheshire's eyes before lifting hers to the royal box of Cards. Seated in the top box, right next to the High King, Hare lounged, one arm flung over the back of his chair. Beside him sat the current High King of Cards—the King of Clovers. This was his third year in a row of being High King.

Lam raised her hand in the salute of Cards: four fingers splayed and thumb curled in, reaching straight into the sky. Lam brought her hand down to her heart, pounding once on her chest to show she was from the Kingdom of Hearts. All the other competitors from Cards did the same, though ending differently to signify their kingdom. Ravine and Ravenel brought their hands back to their foreheads; Myla and Aldwin brought theirs back to their shoulders; and Wesley brought his hand to his cheek. Lam was most interested to see Cheshire, as he didn't belong to any one kingdom, but he simply brought his hand back to his heart and knocked his chest twice, showing he was not born to Hearts, but it was his kingdom. It was strangely touching and painfully striking that she hadn't noticed it when she herself had sat in the royal box just the year before.

Had he also claimed he was a child of Hearts the year before and she just hadn't noticed? Had he done something different? The words of the Tweedles snapped her eyes and thoughts back to the arena as she spun to catch Teon's waiting gaze, blank as newly smoothed marble. Something black was poking out from under his armor, a mark running down his neck, dark as a fresh tattoo. Her eyes flicked past him to see the other members of Chess complete their salutes —one hand grazing the side of their face, palm out, the other forming a fist on the opposite side of the chest. Both Red and White Chess had the same salute, but done as mirrors of each other.

"We will call—"

"Out the names—"

"Of two contestants—"

"Who will then—"

"Walk to the center—"

"Of the playing field." Deevon held to make sure they all understood.

"The match will end—"

"When one—"

"Or both—"

"Of the contestants—"

"Are in a fatal position," Day paused, leaving room for questions.

"The first two contestants are—"

"Lamprocapnos S. Heart and—"

"Vala Y. Marble."

Smoothly, Lam pulled her axe from her back as she stepped to the center. The noise of the crowd was pushed to the back of her mind as her eye sharpened. The lines of the female bishop's armor, the glint of its brightness, all became clear and distinct as Lam let out a breath. Unconsciously, she began to swing her axe, blood starting to pool in her cheeks. Vala's eyes tracked the blade, too caught in the light reflected off it to notice its approach. Abruptly, Lam stopped the blade, inches from Vala's neck, and held out her hand.

A smile playing on her lips and cheers in her ears, Lam shook the bishop's hand. Vala blinked down at Lam, her gaze shadowed by something Lam didn't recognize.

"You…" Fear hid in Vala's eyes, and she dropped Lam's hand, turning her back and waiting for match would begin.

A thick taste of insult coated Lam's tongue as she, too, turned. A cloak of clawing disappointment pulled at Lam's back as the Tweedles blew their horns once more.

The two girls took four steps from one another before turning back and bowing. The horn blew through the crowd, the peoples' cheers signaling the beginning of the match as much as the Tweedles. Her eyes rose to catch Vala holding two daggers connected by a wire.

Lam cursed the distance between them and rushed forward. Vala tilted her head, watching Lam's feet before moving at impossible speeds. The smooth pain of a barbed dagger entering skin sounded in Lam's left bicep. Before Vala could pull it back, Lam wrapped the wire around her arm and hand. Gold cut Lam's vision into pieces, possibilities, strings of fate she was now ripping. Her hand tightened and she wrenched the wire towards herself. Blood spurted from the girl's hands as the second dagger sliced Vala's palm.

The bishop stumbled, not used to the pain shooting up her body, leaving Lam enough time to get into her guard and place her axe to Vala's neck.

The horns sounded, and fear flashed over Vala's face. Her eyes jumped to the Chess stands as she whispered, "I need to do more." With wild eyes, Vala lifted her free dagger and stabbed it into Lam's left forearm.

Shouts of rage and outcries of injustice sounded from the Cards' side of the arena.

This time when the horns blew, it was three blasts in quick succession, reporting that foul play had been committed. Vala was escorted from the field, and Lam was seen by an active nurseturtium. She was only allowed to take out the second knife and heal the wound, seeing as the other had been dealt fairly during the game.

'I need to do more.'

Lam's mind ran over the words as blood ran down her arm. While the nurse walked away, Lam dug her fingers around the knife and ripped out the barbed blade. Proud chants fell on deaf ears as Lam walked to the victor's side of the arena. There was something terribly wrong about the world, about the way Vala had looked to the stands, about the way there was a chill in the air on a fine spring day.

"Next," hesitation was thick in Day's voice.

"Cheshire C. Cheshire and," Devon was calmer, but there was something shaken in her words.

"Adelyn W. Queenside."

The two walked from their respective sides, Cheshire tossing up his weapon and catching it as Adelyn pulled on a pair of brass knuckles. The weapon had sparked much debate when the princess had first started using them over the past year, but her dedication to the rings never faltered. It was strange for Lam to think that their odd choices in weapons was another connection between them. Across the field, their eyes met and again a line of black caught Lam's attention. Despite the full white and gold armor the princess wore, twisting black lines could be seen snaking out from under her forearm guards. With a flick of her head, Adelyn broke eye contact, and Lam turned to see the side of Cheshire's face, mostly covered by his hood. She could feel the strength of his glare even from where she stood. When the horn blew, Lam caught Cheshire's eyes, black and menacing as the weapons in their hands.

"Spades' speed." She wasn't sure why the saying moved her lips, but even with the distance between them, Cheshire seemed to read her mouth and nodded.

Four steps, four beats of her heart, all in only one breath. Then the horn blew again and blood hit the stands.

Both Adelyn and Cheshire had ripped through skin. Cheshire had sliced into her calf, reopening her wound from the second game, as one of Adelyn's metal-bound fists had slammed into his jaw. Flicking his head, Cheshire spat blood to the ground as he grabbed Adelyn's fist.

"Come on, come on, come on—" Lam wasn't sure when she'd started chanting, when her heart had started to beat to her lips and to her hands, cracking knuckles.

Cheshire spun into Adelyn, pulling his weapon back and slicing her leg while he slammed his elbow into the taller girl's stomach and smacked her in the face with the back of his head. His opponent dazed, Cheshire was able to stab down and into Adelyn's foot, pinning her to the ground. With a twist of his hands, the weapon split into two, one half still stabbed though her foot and the other then held at her neck, ending the second match.

Pumping her fist, Lam cheered with the rest of Cards at Cheshire's victory. As he walked over, Lam saw his eyes shift from black to green to a bright, shining yellow.

"You're almost acting like you thought I'd loose."

Lam punched his arm lightly. "And if I did?"

"Then you, dear," he shook his head, "would be quite the fool."

A shiver shook Lam's body as she dropped her arm. Suddenly, she felt eyes on her and the phantom weight of coins in her hand. "Don't call me a fool." The chill had run over her tongue and out of her mouth.

Cheshire looked up sharply, orange coating his eyes. "I—"

The sound of horns cut him off as Rudyard and Ember were called to face one another.

Completely blindsided, Lam twisted to see her brother, slack-jawed and staring across the field. Ember, too, stared at the announcers, as if checking for a mistake that had not been made.

Hesitantly, the two royals moved towards each other. Rudyard's sword swung limply by his side and Lam was surprised to see Ember also trailing a sword. Her body was clothed in a wolf's hide over her red plate armor, her head covered by a wolf-style helm, mouth open to let her stare into the eyes of the Prince of Hearts. When they met in the center, silent words were exchanged between them before they turned.

One, two, three, four. The footsteps seemed loud in the silence. A pause held court, followed by the blow of two horns.

The two turned and bowed, Ember going so far as to curtsy. Somehow, as the horns rang out again, it felt more like the start of a dance. Their blades clanged against one another, carrying the beat of the song. Every time gold met steel, a lightness filled Lam, but it was the lightness of falling, and it ripped the air from her lungs.

It was a painful sort of beauty and agonizing to watch. Blades sparked and fear struck their eyes.

Mutters began to fill the stands as the match dragged on. Lam wished she could tell them all to shut up. Couldn't they see how much pain and love coated her brother? ...how hard it was for both of the fighting royals?

"Finish it!" The words boomed over the stands and Lam's eye were forced to the Queen of Red Chess, the woman draped in a blood red pelt. Her fists were clenched and annoyance bled from her as she stared at her daughter. "Any child of mine can do better than that."

Ember shook her head, but pushed Rudyard harder. His feet stumbled back, but he caught her strike and twisted her sword from her hands. With his blade at her chest and hers out of reach, the third match came to an end. Both bowed and the queen angrily fell back into her chair. With a confident grace, Rudyard walked to the sword, lifted it, and presented it to his love with a bow. Their hands met, through metal and silence, a whole conversation passed between them, perhaps even a confession, then his hand fell away, and they turned their backs on one another. Rudyard barely nodded at Lam as she patted his shoulder when he reached the winning side.

"Next,"

"Teon S. Wystan and—"

"Ravine E. Spade."

The two met in the middle and neither faked politeness. Ravine not bowing was standard, but Teon... Lam focused and noticed there was something off about him, something too tight about the way he held himself.

Like Cheshire, Ravine stared at Lam as the horn blew. Then she slammed a night-black helm on her head and flicked out her sharpened, metal fans.

Teon barely waited for the horn to sound again before he spun and slashed his spear down. Ravine was able to catch it between the notches of her fan and run under his guard. Barely too late, Ravine slashed with her free fan as Teon caught her chest with his free arm. She was thrown at least four feet, her back arching at the impact. Flipping his spear, Teon seemed to teleport to her and stab down through her right shoulder, his blade inches from her neck.

The crowd erupted into gasps and cheers. Before the Tweedles could get the horns to their their lips, Teon had pulled his spear out and stabbed into her low abdomen. Blood, so thick it looked black, was torn from her, a gasping moan of pain.

"What th—"

"You're dead!"

Even from where Lam stood, the sheer rage coming off of Ravenel was enough to pull her muscles taught. People tried to pull his arms down as he stared and pulled out his throwing knives. Ravenel was a master of guns, but he was skilled enough with knives to make Lam's blood rush cold.

"Your name will be on the scrolls of Underland before the sun sets! You—"

Someone grabbed his face and pushed him back.

Lam's fear was drowned by the cries of the stands. All of the people from Spades in attendance rose to their feet and filled in the curses Ravenel wasn't allowed to say. A sea of White and Red stood to their feet, calmly stating that Teon was within his rights as wicked smiles belied their sentiment.

Teon, for his part, merely flicked his spear and walked towards Lam. Heart heavy in her chest, Lam stepped back and towards Cheshire.

As he slowed to a stop, he spoke softly, "I can take you out of here."

Lam stared at Ravine, and she stared back as her helm was removed. Slowly, as nurseturtiums lifted her up, she raised her bloody arm and mouthed, 'Blood in the water.'

Lam turned from her bleeding friend and to the boy who'd asked for her hand. "I don't think I ever want you to take me anywhere." Anger twisted her voice and her face. "And just because it wasn't called, doesn't mean you didn't fight disgustingly."

His face hardened and stared down at her. "All's fair in love and war." Then he moved from her and leaned on the wall.

Every piece of the world seemed tense as Saxon and Wesley were called to the center. Lam saw the bishop's eyes flick to the stands and this time she could see where Vala had been looking. Though the royal box of Chess was almost directly behind him, he stared at it, the seat slightly off to the right. Wesley bowed hopefully, but Saxon only turned from him and bowed to his royals.

Wesley, fighting with his twin short swords, was far better than Lam remembered, but the bishop was feral. Wesley ran in and swept up with one of his swords. The blade made contact with Saxon's armpit. Seeming not to notice, Saxon stepped back, dragging the blade and pulling blood from the wound. Once he was far enough, Saxon raised his whip. The weapon looked wrong in his hands—too brutal, too much. There was a sharp crack as the barbed leather scored Wesley's arm, then his leg, then his foot, leaving deep gashes. Saxon's aim was pathetic, but everything landed at such close range.

Wesley stumbled forward and barely got his blades to the bishop's neck before the match was called and both were carried to the losing side.

Lam had only ever attended one game to observe. It had been the year before, and it paled in comparison to this. Chess was know for being ruthless, but today they were unnecessarily brutal. More blood than sand seemed to coat the top of the field.

Delicately, Lam ran her hands over the gashes in her arm.

"What do you want?" She wasn't asking the joker beside her, or Teon behind her, but the prince staring down at her form high above. Her lips cured as she stared at Zacharie. "Why?"

"Next—"

"Ravenel A. Spade and—"

"Elfin I. Kingside."

Elfin held her head high as she walked to the center, while Ravenel didn't even raise his to look at her. He, like his sister, wore a black helm, but his only covered the lower half of his face and head, leaving a large slit for his eyes. Once again, the two didn't bow. Ravenel didn't look at the victors as he turned, only stared at the two knives in his hands.

Before the horn had even finished blowing, a wet whisper met the cacophony. Ravenel hadn't won the last game with luck, and it wasn't luck that buried his blade in the princess's heart. Elfin stood stunned a moment, and so did the crowd, as fiery red dripped from her chest. Shaking hands slowly rose to cover the hole and Ravenel stared at the Royals of Chess. Then he flung his second knife into the sand before them and walked to the winning side.

Madness broke out as shouts and objections were hurled down at the prince. Despite the desperate blows of the horns, it took over twenty minutes for Chess to calm down, twenty minutes for Lam to stare in shock at the dying princess. Somehow, in the first minute, Hare had jumped down from the box and rushed to crouch beside her. Holding the girl, he fed her a deep black-blue potion that was slipping out of her gasping mouth far more than running down her throat. The princess's eyes were brimming with tears even as they started to drift closed. Elfin didn't fall gently; she shook and moaned as her strength stained the scales of her armor.

Tick.

Tick.

Tick.

Heartbeats and seconds mixed together as Lam stared at the dying girl. The only thing she could think was: *The horn had sounded, your opponent was mad, you should have expected the blow.* She wanted to be kind, be gentle, but... *'If not our blood, then whose?'*

It wasn't her lying there, it wasn't her heart melting into the sand, and for that, she was thankful. At some point, she had grabbed Cheshire's hand, his fingers intertwined with hers. He wasn't the one on the sand. Rudyard grabbed her undamaged arm. It wasn't him dying now. They were cruel thoughts, but it was all she had.

A hand shot out and grabbed Lam by the arm so hard she flinched. "Listen closely. If we lose focus, it will be one of us lying on that ground." Ravenel's words bit into Lam, leaving her slack-jawed and wide-eyed.

She knew all of that...but not in that way, not told by a prince who had blood on his hands from that very game, not looking over his shoulder to see Teon watching her with an emotionless depth.

"Do you hear me?" the prince's voice was a whisper, slicing his tongue.

"I understand."

Ravenel's hand fell from her arm, his fingers red from where they'd pressed into the sharp metal. "Then may the King win."

Twisting, Lam caught Cheshire's eyes. "And the Fool find his path." Purple was thick in his gaze and heavy on her shoulders, heavy in her chest.

Standing and shouting for help, Hare rushed Elfin to proper medical care, desperately trying to keep the royal from dying. When the crowd finally settled down, the horns were blown for the final match of the first round which, sadly, was between Aldwin and Myla.

Few in the crowd not from Clovers cared at all, and no one was surprised when Aldwin was the victor. He'd simply knocked her butterfly sword from her hands and held on to his morning star. No damage was done, and neither of them contributed to the blood on the earth.

All of their names were set into a gold chalice and each one of the Tweetle's arms grabbed a slip of paper.

"Lamprocapnos S. Heart and—"

Days face lit in surprise and her eye flicked up to them as she spoke, "Cheshire C. Cheshire."

Lam stared blankly, noticing she was still holding Cheshire's hand at her side. Smoothly, he pulled it from her grip, his face still shrouded by his hood. He made it to the center before Lam even moved, turning to face her with not a hint of expression on his face. His eyes shown white, something Lam had never seen, something she couldn't read.

Stalking forward, she grabbed her axe—she wasn't sure when she had sheathed it—and moved to stand back-to-back with him.

"I'm sorry, but I can't go easy on you here." His voice was bland and low.

Lam shook her head. "I won't either."

"I would be more disappointed if you did." The humor in his voice pulled a smile from her.

The call of the horns rang out at they took only two steps, as was customary for the second round.

Lam turned to find the king of death staring at her with lovely, white eyes. Shivers racked her body, and she almost didn't hear the horns.

Before she could think, her body had already taken over.

Images ran though her—tactics, possibilities, the gold lines that seemed to cluster around Cheshire more than they did around anyone else. Her axe swung up and caught Cheshire's blade before slamming it to the ground. A fire Lam had only ever tasted sparked in every inch of her body. Her cheeks flushed bright red, and a smile tore her lips. With Cheshire's blade still buried, Lam ran forward and cut a gash along his arm. Pain shot through his eyes, disrupting the white with streaks of purple. Swiftly, Lam spun as Cheshire pulled his weapon from the earth. Lam felt the bite of an animal as his blade crashed into her back. Blood thick and as dark as treacle ran from her as she turned back to him.

Their weapons met in the middle. Black and gold, sparking in the midday sun, trailing more of the gold that only she could see. Lam slipped under and swung to meet his leg. Blocking, Cheshire stepped back, leaving his weapon in an unstable position. Lam sprang back to standing and flipped his blade from his grip. White switched to orange and Lam's blade was held next to his neck.

Why did she stop?

Her smile twitched and fell as her thoughts registered with the sane part of her brain. Why had she gone so far? The horns called Lam's victory, rippling the now fading gold lines, but Lam just stood, struck immovable by her own emotions. What had she just done?

Eyes shifting from purple to blue, Cheshire stepped back, letting her axe hang in empty air. Then he turned and walked away. Unlike the others, he didn't leave or go to the stands. Instead, he sat in the Cards' tunnel. Straightening, Lam turned, bowed to her royals, and walked to stand next to her brother.

As Lam returned to normal, an overwhelming sense of fear sank into her. Her whole body twisted to Cheshire, his eyes still glinting at her from the shadows, only twelve yards away. Slouching, he gave her a smile and clapped. Lam felt some of the weight in her chest lifted, but...

I could have killed him.

Her blood had felt hot and the world seemed to be at her fingertips. Strings of Fate had been as strong as spiderwebs in those moments, and ice had held her eyes open. A darkness—a beast inside her—seemed to be stretching from its sleep and starting to rear its head.

"Next,"

Her eyes returned to the Tweedles.

"Aldwin K. Clovers, and—"

"Ravenel A. Spade."

The two princes moved to the center, Ravenel wielding the knives that had been retrieved for him and Aldwin swinging his morning star. Both bowed to each other before turning back to back and waiting for the signal. Even as the sun rose high in the sky, the air stayed oddly cold, as if Spring was afraid to breathe.

One call, two steps. Spring wasn't the only one holding its breath as the young kings turned and began to step in a circular manner. Aldwin held the advantage at mid range, but Ravenel had proven himself to be a far better fighter. Their feet mapped a perfect ring, boots sinking into the blood-soaked ground. It all was starting to smell like blood, the near-death choking Lam's breath. Still, for some horrific reason she herself did not understand, her face flushed and her heart beat faster. On the field, gold strings spread, even with her eyes open, spoiling the match to come. She saw the lines that Ravenel would trace, his body sliding past the spiked mace that would scrape against his shoulder. Her heart beat harder, her vision turning red. The more they circled, the clearer the lines got, the closer time ticked. Never before had she seen the gold this clearly. It exhilarated and disturbed her all at once. She couldn't help but twitch her fingers, tapping them along with the beat of Ravenel's boots, crescendoing as his blade poised at Aldwin's neck.

"Next,"

Lam followed the gloved fingers of Day and Devon as they lifted two more names.

"Rudyard M. Heart, and—"

"Teon S. Wystan."

It felt all wrong to Lam as they walked to the middle. It wasn't right. Like the electric charge right before a lighting strike. She was so close to calling out, to stop the match, but... she couldn't speak. Teon caught her eyes, and Lam felt her heart stop. They held nothing, just a blank slate, a shear cliff of stone.

"Run, Lam!"

No one seemed to hear the call. Only Lam turned to the woman with red hair and a gold crown, staring down at Lam with shining eyes. "Run from your fate." Why was the young woman scared? Why did she look exactly like her? Why did fate have to play with her so much?

Before any horn could sound, Teon twisted around, stepped forward, and placed his arms around Rudyard's neck. It happened so fast, the open palm facing out away from Rudyard's cheek, the other arm curving behind his neck, holding a white spear, then a heavy, thick, impossible snap.

Tick.

Tick.

Tick.

Even the Storytellers held their breath as Teon turned the lolling head of Rudyard to face Lam. Her brother's eyes were red, his skin a light cream, a spray of freckles dotted his forehead. Lam's brother wouldn't sag, he wouldn't leave his mouth hanging open or his eyes staring blankly at the bloody ground. Her brother wouldn't lose control of his body, he wouldn't stop— he wouldn't... die. But the Prince of Hearts did all of that then.

The yell she would shout a thousand times remembering this moment could not yet come. Her hands formed a bird cage around her mouth, something delicate and hollow, ready to break down when she was told it was a joke. The Knight of White Chess finished his salute to the Kings and Queens of Cards, pulling his arms away and letting the prince crash to his knees. Rudyard stayed there for a moment, limp arms brushing the ground, head bowed in front of his parents, his peers, his kingdom. Then the prince, who would never be king, tipped.

Teon stared up at the the Royals of Cards, eyes glinting with nothing as a swirling black mark forced its fingers higher up his neck. Raising his spear, he pointed at the High King. The crowd was silent as this broken boy challenged the King and the entire Deck of Cards.

The knight raised his chin, his voice saying words that were not his own. "Chess has issued a new game." As one, the Kings and Queens of Chess rose behind their champion.

There was something maniacal in Zacharie's face as he clapped his hands and looked down at Lam. "Ring around the Rosie..."

Lam was suddenly ten and Zacharie was humming as he lit matches and dropped them at the feet of one of the servant girls in the palace of Hearts. Everything fell away, overlayed by the twin voices of the young and old prince singing, his voice somehow running through the stadium.

"Pocket full of posies..."

But there was another song too, a rhyme, a warning. The Prince of White Chess had always been impossibly pale, but now he was as white as dried bones...save for the black lines snaking down his arms.

'Blood Weavers white as snow,
Black lines come, magic goes,
The lines will shine
The lines will fade,
The white a sign,
That magic waits.'

"Ashes,"

His hands ceased their clapping and gripped the rail in front of him. The black lines, starting at his shoulders, reached down to his fingers.

"Ashes,"

Horror and white flames were starting to run over the railings, blooming in the stands. It filled her lungs and Cheshire was screaming something at her as countless others started to scream as well.

"You all fall down."

An explosion rocked the world as half the arena burst into flame, ripping humanity into two once again.

Tears were burning their way down Lam's face, but she couldn't stop staring at Zacharie.

His grin grew as he shook his head and mouthed, "You never keep your eyes on what matters."

PART TWO
THE WAR

Blood was always the hardest thing to look at,
and where my eyes were always drawn.
So do not blame me for staring at your blood on my chest.
Please lover, for me: don't stare at my dead form.
-The Queen of Wonderland

www.ingramcontent.com/pod-product-compliance
Lightning Source LLC
Chambersburg PA
CBHW060711190726

48289CB00002B/630